KT-557-058

'There's a telegram for you, Lacey,' called Benton, a club instructor, who came out of the office as he passed.

'Telegram for me?' cried Algy in amazement. 'Who on earth—' He took the buff envelope and tore it open impatiently. It was addressed simply, *Algy Lacey, Brooklands Aerodrome.*

'Come at once, bring machine, Biggles captured. Waiting for you at Cramlington Aerodrome.
                                                Ginger.'

Captain W. E. Johns was born in Hertfordshire in 1893. He flew with the Royal Flying Corps in the First World War and made a daring escape from a German prison camp in 1918. Between the wars he edited *Flying* and *Popular Flying* and became a writer for the Ministry of Defence. The first Biggles story, *Biggles the Camels are Coming* was published in 1932, and W. E. Johns went on to write a staggering 102 Biggles titles before his death in 1968.

www.kidsatrandomhouse.co.uk

BIGGLES BOOKS
PUBLISHED IN THIS EDITION

BIGGLES
and the
BLACK PERIL

CAPTAIN W.E. JOHNS

RED FOX

Red Fox would like to express their grateful thanks
for help given in the preparation of these editions to Jennifer Schofield,
author of *By Jove, Biggles*, Linda Shaughnessy of A. P. Watt Ltd
and especially to the late John Trendler.

BIGGLES AND THE BLACK PERIL
A RED FOX BOOK 1 86 230224 3

First published in Great Britain by John Hamilton, 1935

This Red Fox edition published 2004

Papers used by Random House Children's Books are natural, recyclable
products made from wood grown in sustainable forests. The manufacturing
processes conform to the environmental regulations of the country of origin.

Red Fox Books are published by Random House Children's Books,
61–63 Uxbridge Road, London W5 5SA,
a division of The Random House Group Ltd,
in Australia by Random House Australia (Pty) Ltd,
20 Alfred Street, Milsons Point, Sydney, NSW 2061, Australia,
in New Zealand by Random House New Zealand Ltd,
18 Poland Road, Glenfield, Auckland 10, New Zealand,
and in South Africa by Random House (Pty) Ltd,
Endulini, 5A Jubilee Road, Parktown 2193, South Africa

THE RANDOM HOUSE GROUP Limited Reg. No. 954009

A CIP catalogue record for this book is available from the British Library.

Printed and bound in Great Britain by
Cox and Wyman Ltd, Reading, Berkshire,

Contents

Chapter 1
Forced Down

The northern horizon, which for some time had been
growing more and more indistinct, finally disappeared, and the dull, greeny-black sea merged into
the grey canopy of the sky. Biggles leaned out of the
cockpit of his Vandal amphibian* aeroplane, pushed
up his goggles, and peered ahead anxiously. For a full
minute he stared, and a frown creased his forehead
as he looked back at Algy Lacey, sitting in the second
pilot's seat beside him.

'I don't like it!' he shouted above the roar of the
engine. 'That stuff'll start coming down presently.' He
jerked his head at the forbidding cloud-mass above.

Algy indicated that he had heard by a grimace of
annoyance. 'Typical English weather,' he reflected.
The sun had been shining from a cloudless, blue,
autumn sky when Biggles had rung him up that morning to suggest a joy-ride, a proposal to which he had
readily agreed. They had travelled by road to Brooklands Aerodrome, where they had parked the amphibian after their return from South America**, and after
a short discussion as to the most desirable route, they
had left the ground shortly after two o'clock.

They had picked up the Thames, followed it as far

---

* A marine aircraft, with a boat-shaped hull for landing on water,
which was also fitted with retractable wheels for use on land.
** See *Biggles Flies Again.*

as the estuary, and then turning north continued up the east coast. It had been their intention to find a suitable cove in which to land if the water was smooth enough, and have a picnic tea from a hamper which reposed in the cabin; alternatively, if the water was choppy, they would turn inland to one of the many north country aerodromes, and land on *terra firma*, leaving the ground in time to get back to Brooklands by dusk, which would be about six o'clock. The change in the weather had first been apparent as they were passing Felixstowe, but Biggles had held on to his course hoping it would improve. On the contrary it had grown steadily worse, until now, with the Wash behind them and the Lincolnshire coast two thousand feet below their keel, it had become definitely forbidding.

A wraith of white mist enveloped the machine with a clammy embrace, and blotted out the landscape. The noise of the engine faded suddenly as Biggles throttled back to lose height, and then sprang to life again as they sank through the vapour and the ground once more appeared below.

'Going back!' he yelled, and suiting the action to the word, swung the machine round and began to retrace his course. His frown deepened as he peered through the windscreen. From east to west, straight across their path, lay a dark, uniform, indigo belt that could only mean rain, and heavy rain at that. Land and sea, at a distance of a mile or two, were swallowed up in gloom. Then, as so often happens in such conditions, the moisture-laden sky above began to close down on them. Twice within five minutes the machine was enveloped in opaque mist, so thick that the wing tips were lost in it, and each time the pilot

8

was compelled to lose height in order to keep the ground in sight. He jerked the throttle wide open, and the bellow of the engine increased in volume as it jumped from cruising to maximum speed; the revolution counter needle vibrated, and crept upwards, and the air speed indicator leapt from ninety miles an hour to a hundred and ten.

They were now recrossing the Wash, and he touched his right rudder slightly in order to strike the coast, their only landmark, as quickly as possible; they were down to five hundred feet when it loomed dimly ahead. At the same moment a sharp spatter of rain struck them; it formed in curious little globules on the doped planes*, tiny beads of moisture that danced towards the trailing edge and then disappeared into space. Visibility quickly grew worse until he could only just see the ground from a hundred feet; so thick was it that at times it was difficult to tell whether land or sea lay below. He pushed his stick** forward a trifle, staring over the side, and saw that they were passing over a little natural creek. The water in it was smooth, for the storm had not yet had time to beat up a big sea, and he made up his mind with the promptness of long experience. The roar of the engine ceased abruptly; the Vandal tilted in a swift 'S' turn, sideslipped, flattened out, and cut a creamy wake across the smooth water of the creek.

'And that's that,' observed Algy philosophically, as the machine ran to a standstill.

* On aircraft where the wings were covered in fabric material, the fabric was coated in a chemical solution called dope to make them waterproof, taut and airproof.
** Slang for control column, a vertical lever or wheel, controlling the fore and aft and lateral movements of the aircraft.

'As you say, that's that,' agreed Biggles, unfastening the strap of his flying cap. 'And I don't mind telling you that I'm not sorry to be on the carpet. Did you ever see visibility cut right out like that in your life?'

'Never.'

'Nor I. Well, we're down and that's something,' went on Biggles. 'I haven't the remotest idea where we are, except that that bit of oozy looking marsh over there is part of Norfolk, and the liquid on which we are floating is the North Sea.'

'What are we going to do?'

'Taxi along this creek until we find a sheltered place to moor up, and then unpack that hamper. One thing I'm not going to do is to take off again in this soup; my goodness! hark at the rain!'

'If it keeps on it looks as if we're here for the night.'

'We are as far as I'm concerned,' declared Biggles, as he opened the throttle a trifle and began taxi-ing along the low, bleak shore. 'Here we are, what about this?'

At the spot indicated, a short, narrow arm of the creek felt its way through wire-grass covered sand-hills that arose here and there from a swampy reed-covered plain.

'Do as well as anywhere,' agreed Algy. 'Go ahead; taxi right in and beach her here. I'll get out and have a look round.' He jumped ashore on firm sand and ran to the top of the nearest sand-hill. He was back again in a moment. 'Nothing,' he said tersely, 'not a blooming thing in sight, although I can't see more than a hundred yards if it comes to that.'

'Well, come back in and let's have some tea; maybe the clouds will lift again presently.'

In this hope they were doomed to disappointment

however, for an hour later, although the rain had stopped, the air was still thick with mist and visibility practically nil. Presently it began to grow dark.

'Nothing doing,' declared Biggles, 'it's clearing, I believe, but I'm not taking a chance. It will be as black as your hat in a few minutes, and night flying with fog about is not my idea of an amusing evening. What the dickens was that?' he went on in alarm, as the machine gave a sudden lurch. He put his head out of the cabin window and then laughed. 'We're a nice pair of fools,' he observed. 'Well, that settles it anyway, we're here for the night now without any argument.'

'Why, what is it?'

'The tide's gone out while we've been sitting here and left us high and dry; even if we could get our wheels down there isn't room to turn. No matter, it's safe anchorage, and we're well protected in this gully. It could blow a gale without hurting us.'

'But what about grub? We look like getting no dinner.'

'What a fellow you are; always thinking about your stomach. Let's get ashore and see if there is a house anywhere in sight. After all, we're in England, and in my experience one can't go far in England without bumping into a house of some sort.'

In this, however, he was not altogether correct, as a close examination of the desolate landscape quickly revealed. In all directions, as far as they could see in the gathering darkness, stretched a monotonous expanse of flat, bleak moorland, in which the receding tide had left sinister-looking rivers of mud. They tried to find a way through them, but quickly gave it up after slipping knee deep in slime at every other step.

'Come on, let's get back to the machine,' said Biggles disgustedly. 'There's no sense in drowning ourselves in this bog.'

'Hold hard a minute, what's that over there?' asked Algy, peering into the gloom.

'I can see what you mean; it's a building of some sort,' returned Biggles.

They picked their way carefully towards it, but their hopes of finding a human habitation were soon dashed to the ground. As they drew near, the building resolved itself into a small, square concrete structure, with a flat roof; a single window, an open unglazed square cut in the wall, overlooked the sea. A wooden door gave access to it on the landward side.

'Cheerful-looking hole,' observed Algy. 'You know a lot, perhaps you can tell me what sort of madman would build a place like that in a place like this, and what for?'

Biggles grinned. 'I think I can tell you that,' he replied. 'It looks like a relic of the War, one of those pillbox* affairs they built all round the coast. They were used as look-out posts or machine-gun emplacements probably, but I'm not quite sure about that. Watch your step for barbed wire and old trenches. They had Territorials** putting up wire entanglements and digging trenches all round the east coast, and in many places, where the ground was not wanted for cultivation, they have been left just as they were at the end of the War. There you are, what did I tell you?' he went on, pointing to a zig-zag depression

---

* A small reinforced concrete hut, used as a defensive position by soldiers.
** Soldiers of the British army, used for local defence.

that wound its way through the sand-hills. On the seaward side of it was a row of rotting stakes and a tangle of barbed wire. 'Yes, this is a bit of the War, there's no doubt of that,' he concluded. 'Come on, let's get back.'

'Wait a minute, we may as well look inside; it might be more comfortable here than in the cabin,' suggested Algy.

'There might be more room, but it will be less cheerful, and colder, I imagine,' replied Biggles, pushing the door open. 'More like a prison cell than anything else,' he went on, striking a match. 'Well, there's nothing here, let's go.'

'Just a minute, strike another match; I saw a piece of candle – it may be useful.'

'Candle!'

'Yes. There's nothing funny about that, is there?'

'No, I suppose not, except that it's odd that a candle should remain here for so long.'

Biggles lighted the candle, of which a good half remained, and they surveyed the blank walls of the deserted building. 'Yes, we shall do better in the cabin,' he said.

'I'm not so sure. If we could get a good fire going—'

'Fire! What are we going to burn.'

'We could burn the door,' suggested Algy brightly.

'Well, go ahead and pick it to pieces with your fingers,' sneered Biggles. 'It would take an axe to make any impression on that.'

'Don't be funny,' Algy told him. 'What's this, I wonder,' he went on, stooping and picking up a small piece of paper that was half buried on the sandy floor. He held it to the candle and a curious expression crept over his face as he looked at it. 'That's funny,' he said.

'What is?'

'If, as you say, this was a British dugout, how comes this here?' questioned Algy, passing him the paper.

'*Gesellschaft Deutsche Gontermann, Berlin,*' read Biggles, turning the paper over. 'Well, I'm dashed. This is a label, and it doesn't look very old.'

'What do you make of it?'

'I don't know what to make of it, unless someone has had some German machinery stored here; a farmer, for instance.'

'I'm not an agricultural expert, but this place doesn't look to me as if much farming has been done around here lately,' replied Algy. 'Has that anything to do with it, I wonder?'

Biggles saw that he was looking at something on the wall, and crossed over to see what it was.

'What about that?' asked Algy.

Someone at some time had drawn a curious device in black paint on the seaward wall. It appeared thus:

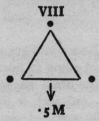

'Beats me,' muttered Biggles, 'unless, it's an Admiralty mark of some sort – that may be it.'

'Reminds me of those plates you see on walls – fire hydrants, aren't they?'

'Yes,' replied Biggles slowly. He put out his hand

and touched the mark; then he withdrew it and looked at his fingers. 'Why, it's wet!' he said in an amazed whisper. 'Someone must use this place, but what on earth for is more than I can imagine unless it is the Admiralty, or the Ministry of Fisheries – if there is such a thing. But one thing is certain; that sign, or whatever you like to call it, means something. By Jove! I believe that hydrant idea of yours was right; those marks mean distance and position. They couldn't mean anything else. That arrow at the bottom, for instance, and the M. If M means "Mile," it means something is half a mile straight down, so obviously that isn't it. What else could it mean besides mile – metre – that's it. Half a metre – just over eighteen inches.'

'Perhaps it's buried treasure?' suggested Algy hopefully.

'Buried fiddlesticks. Wait a minute,' Biggles began stamping about on the floor. 'Here it is, whatever it is,' he announced, as the solid sound suddenly gave way to a hollow one. 'Just where you picked up that piece of paper. Find a piece of wood or something to dig with. This is rather fun; we've nothing else to do so it will kill time.'

Algy hunted about with the candle outside the door, and presently returned with an old rusty piece of iron.

'That'll do,' declared Biggles, and began scraping away the earth from the hollow place.

Ten minutes later, taking it in turns, they struck something solid, and, raking aside the loose earth with their hands, exposed an iron manhole cover.

'Gold!' chortled Algy. 'I've always wanted to find a miser's hoard – strewth!'

The exclamation leapt to his lips as Biggles lifted

15

the cover, exposing what lay beneath. What Algy seriously expected to find he did not know, but it was certainly not what he now saw. At first glance it appeared to be a complicated piece of machinery, but a close examination showed it to be a row of large electric accumulators,* some intricate wiring, and a switch.

'Here, we'd better cover this up; it's an Admiralty gadget all right; must be,' said Biggles seriously.

'What about switching on the switch to see what happens?'

'Don't be a fool, anything might happen. That switch might explode a mine-field somewhere and blow the fleet up for all we know.'

'Admiralty my foot!' cried Algy suddenly, bending down. 'The Admiralty don't use German machines, do they?'

'I shouldn't think so, why?'

'Look at the name on these accumulators.'

'*Gontermann. Berlin.* That's the name that was on the paper. Why, of course,' went on Biggles excitedly, 'that label was on the package that brought this stuff over. But we'd better cover this up; whoever it belongs to it's no concern of ours.'

They set to work and in a few minutes had replaced the soil; when they stood up the ground was as smooth as when they entered the hut.

'Come on, it's time we got back to the machine,' said Biggles, blowing out the candle. 'Crumbs! Isn't it dark, watch your step.'

The lapping of the water on the beach guided them towards the sea, and they had almost reached the

* Rechargeable electric batteries.

Vandal when Biggles laid his hand on Algy's arm. 'Hark!' he said. 'Do I hear a machine, or am I crazy?'

'It's an aeroplane all right,' declared Algy, with his head on one side.

'The mist has cleared, and so has most of the cloud, but who on earth would be night flying on such a night as this?' asked Biggles in surprise. 'What a funny sound the engine makes; sounds sort of muffled. By Jingo, it's coming this way, too,' he went on as the sound drew nearer. 'Stand still a minute and see if the engine tells us anything.'

They stood quite still in the darkness, listening.

'Well, I'm dashed if I know,' he growled, 'but if it was daylight I should say there was a formation of machines upstairs; if there aren't several engines up there I'll eat my hat.'

'Big R.A.F. bomber perhaps?'

'The only Service bombers we have are fitted with Rolls Kestrels or Napier Lions, and those we can hear are certainly neither of those. There are half a dozen engines at least, and we've nothing that size in this country.'

'Two or three machines doing exercises perhaps.'

'Must be; can't be anything else as far as I can see. I—'

'Well, I'm dashed,' interrupted Algy breathlessly.

'What's wrong now?'

'There's a light in the hut – or there was. It's gone now.'

'You're getting light-headed.'

'Light-headed my eye. Do you suppose I don't know what a light is when I see it? I saw a light in that window I tell you, as if someone had flashed an electric torch.'

17

'Impossible!'

'There you are, what did I tell you!' cried Algy triumphantly as the window of the hut became a square of dull orange light. 'Someone's lit that candle.'

'We're beginning to see things,' muttered Biggles. 'What the dickens is happening. Come on, let's go back; whoever it is will be able to tell us where we are, and tell us the way to the nearest village. Hark! By James, that machine has cut off its engines, which knocks your suggestion on the head. If there is more than one machine, the chances against all the pilots throttling back at the identical instant are too remote to be considered. There is only one machine up there and it's a multi-engined job. But never mind that; let's go and see who it is in the hut.'

They hurried back towards the building, and Biggles, from a distance of about a hundred yards, was about to hail the mysterious occupant, when an event occurred, or rather a series of events, that turned their thought into very different channels, and warned them for the first time that they were on dangerous ground.

The first indication of this was a deep reverberating roar that swept through the night a few hundred feet above their heads. Biggles clutched Algy by the arm.

'Great Jumping Jupiter,' he gasped, 'that kite's coming in to land or I'm a Dutchman. What the – get down, quick!'

The last ejaculation had been forced from his lips by an occurrence that was almost paralysing in its unexpectedness, yet the speed with which his warning to take cover had been followed by both of them showed that their brains had not lost their wartime

18

alertness. As Biggles muttered the words they had dived into an old grass covered trench from which they gazed speechlessly at the phenomenon.

The water of the creek had turned to a sea of shimmering liquid fire, green in the centre, with red edges. The effect was unearthly, but as their eyes became accustomed to it they began to understand. The creek had been flood-lit, apparently from below. In the centre the light was probably white, but glowed pale green through the water. A circle of ruby lights marked the boundaries. The meaning of it all may not have been apparent to a landsman, but to an airman the matter needed no explanation. The creek had become an illuminated aerodrome, on which the machine above them was about to land. This assumption proved correct, for within a moment or two the invisible aeroplane could be heard approaching again from the direction of the sea. Biggles caught his breath and Algy stifled an exclamation as a gigantic shadow loomed up just beyond the submarine beacons and dropped majestically on to the creek; as the keel touched, the water became a living, leaping sheet of phosphorescence. The huge machine turned slowly and began to taxi towards the shore; as it did so, as suddenly as they had appeared, every light was extinguished. An instant later a single beam of light leapt from the nose of the slowly taxi-ing machine; it settled on the bank, swept up and down it once or twice, and was in turn extinguished. Only a faint luminous glow from the cockpit marked the position of the giant stranger.

A hail rang out; it was answered instantly from the hut, and a light began to jerk its way towards the beach.

'Don't move,' whispered Biggles, 'the fellow in the hut is coming down to meet them. Now we know what that switch was for. Hark!' A sound of low voices reached them from the direction of the hut. 'There's more than one of them – sounds as if there may be two,' he whispered. 'Keep still, this is interesting.'

Two figures loomed up, one carrying an electric lantern, and passed them at a distance of not more than ten yards. Presently a sound of greetings being exchanged came from the beach.

'It's a good thing the Vandal is out of sight round the corner,' muttered Biggles, 'or that *would* have put the lid on it.'

'What's going on do you think?' whispered Algy. 'Smuggling?'

'Looks like it – on a big scale, too. That machine is a foreigner; I can just make her out. Looks as big as the Do.X.* There's something fishy here and no mistake; I've never even seen a picture of such a machine, so where it has come from goodness alone knows – S-s-h.'

Voices, speaking a foreign language, were approaching, this time from the direction of the water. The faint light in the cockpit disappeared, as if the electrical equipment for illuminating the instrument board had been switched off, and in a moment or two, five figures, walking in single file, loomed up in the night. They disappeared in the direction of the hut and the light reappeared at the window.

'Listen, laddie,' whispered Biggles, 'we've got to see

* The German-manufactured Dornier X Flying Boat. First flown in 1929, powered by twelve engines and designed to carry 72 passengers in comfort, only three were made.

more of this. I'm going down to get a closer view of that machine; we may never get such a chance again. I'll find out its nationality, anyway. You creep up towards the hut and see if you can learn anything, but for the love of Mike don't be seen. I shan't come back here; I'll make for the Vandal – you do the same.' He crawled out of the trench and disappeared into the darkness.

Algy lay still for a few minutes, listening, and then began to creep stealthily towards the hut. It was not difficult to approach unseen, for the night was dark, and the grass covered sand beneath his feet deadened the sound of his footsteps. At a distance of about ten yards he again stopped to listen. He could hear voices distinctly, but they were speaking in a language he did not understand, so the conversation conveyed nothing to him. Dare he risk a peep through the window? It was taking a big risk, and he knew it, for if any one of the five occupants happened to be looking in that direction, he could hardly fail to see him. He decided to take the risk; one glance at the mysterious voyagers might prove invaluable. He wormed his way to the dark side of the hut and then crept across to the base of the concrete wall. So far so good. Crouching low, he rounded the corner, and crept along until he was immediately below the square of light. Then, slowly, and with infinite care, he began to rise. The voices sounded desperately close, and in spite of his efforts to still it, his heart pounded violently; it was a form of thrill that he had never before experienced. Inch by inch his head rose towards the corner of the light; then it drew level, and he took in the scene at a single glance.

The five men were in the room. One, in a heavy

leather flying coat, was holding up a map, which Algy recognized at once as Europe, on the opposite wall; the others were looking closely at it while he spoke. Two of them, obviously the crew of the flying boat, wore sheepskin thigh boots and thick woollen sweaters. The other two, evidently the men who had come overland, wore ordinary lounge suits and overcoats. One was a thin, emaciated-looking fellow with a large nose, like the beak of a bird of prey; the other was inclined to be stout, had a straw coloured moustache and wore a bowler hat. There was nothing outstanding about him; he was of a type that could be seen at any place any time of the day.

The man in the leather coat was obviously the leader, for the others were listening attentively and respectfully as he tapped upon the map with a pencil to emphasize his words. As Algy watched, he placed the point of the pencil on a spot which he had no difficulty in recognizing as the Norfolk coast; probably the very spot on which they now stood. Then, with a swift movement, he swept the pencil across the North Sea to a spot on the eastern side of the Baltic. Several other lines had been drawn on the map from the same spot to various points on the east coast of England, but before Algy could memorize them, the man, of whose face Algy could see nothing except the point of a black beard, took down the map and began to fold it up. They all turned towards the middle of the room and Algy sank down silently.

Not until he was on his hands and knees did he realize how great had been the strain of his surreptitious peep, for he was trembling, and his heart seemed to be up in his throat. He crept like a wraith to the cover of a sand-dune as the door creaked and lay still as death while the light went out and the voices faded away into the night. For perhaps twenty minutes he remained thus, and then, deciding that the coast was clear, began to feel his way cautiously in the direction of the Vandal. He was about half way when the engines of the great flying boat were started up; they swelled into a deep, vibrating hum that receded swiftly into the distance. 'So she's gone off again,' he mused, as he continued on his way. 'I wonder if those other two chaps have gone with it.'

He reached the Vandal and gave a low whistle. There was no reply, so deciding that Biggles had not yet returned, he went aboard and made himself comfortable in the cabin. Half an hour passed slowly and he began to get anxious; at the end of an hour he was definitely alarmed. He jumped down on to the beach and listened; not a sound broke the deathly silence. No light showed in the direction of the hut.

'Biggles!' he called, not too loudly.

There was no reply.

'Biggles!' he called again, raising his voice.

Still no reply.

Something like panic seized him, and casting discretion to the winds, 'Biggles!' he yelled at the top of his voice.

Silence.

An icy hand seemed to clutch his heart, for he knew that the cry must have been heard by anyone within half a mile. He ran to the top of the nearest sand-dune and stood staring into the darkness towards the creek. The moon appeared suddenly from behind a cloud-bank and flooded the scene with silvery radiance. Nothing moved. Not a sound broke the silence of the night. 'Biggles! Hi, Biggles!' he yelled again. There was no answer.

Filled with a nameless horror he began to run towards the beach where the strange aeroplane had been, searching to right and left as he ran. He found footmarks in the sand by the water's edge, but nothing more. For an hour he hunted, looking for what he hoped he would not find, the dead or unconscious body of his friend. At last, weary and unnerved, he sat down on a dune overlooking the sea. 'What could have happened?' he asked himself a hundred times. Could Biggles have fallen into one of the mud swamps and been drowned? Could he have entered the water to examine the aircraft and been carried away by the receding tide? He did not know. Grey dawn came and found him still alone on the edge of the salt marsh. Before him stretched the sea, cold and deserted. Behind lay the waste of barren land, a vast featureless expanse soul-destroying in its utter solitude. At one place only on the far horizon was there a sign of man's presence; the dilapidated arm of an ancient windmill flung a gaunt finger skyward. The only sound was the plaintive cry of the seabirds.

He rose wearily to his feet, suddenly aware that he was very cold, and made his way to the hut, but it was precisely as they had found it the preceding day. 'Well, it's no use staying here,' he muttered bitterly, 'I might as well take the machine back to Brooklands.' He started the engine, climbed into his seat and took off; yet he could not tear himself away from the place. Somewhere there, either in the water, or – he grew cold at the thought – buried under the mud, was Biggles. For half an hour he cruised to and fro, cross-ing and recrossing his track a hundred times, but there was no sign of the man who was tied to him by bonds of friendship that only years of peril could forge. Suddenly making up his mind he swung the machine round, and with a lump in his throat headed south.

Chapter 2
Ginger Takes A Hand

When Biggles left Algy in order to make a closer inspection of the mysterious flying boat, he had little idea of what he was literally walking into. Had the giant aeroplane been a British machine, he would have put the whole thing down to a secret operation being carried out by the Air Ministry, possibly with the co-operation of the Navy, but quite apart from the aeroplane, the fact that the crew were foreigners discountenanced this theory at once. That the nocturnal visitors were engaged in some nefarious scheme was obvious, and he considered it his duty to find out, if possible, just what it was. If it was smuggling, then it was being done on a very large scale, but if that was the case, why had not the crew brought the contraband ashore, for there could be no object in the visit unless a consignment of illicit cargo was to be unloaded. The men who had gone up to the hut were empty handed, he was sure of that, and if the size of the machine was any indication, its pay-load was in order of two or three tons – certainly far more than the meagre crew could unload before dawn.

It was not until he was within a cable's length* of the machine that he fully realized how huge it was, and crouching low on the ground he examined it with a professional eye. It was a metal flying boat of

* Approximately 183 metres.

the high-wing monoplane type, not unlike the famous Dornier Do.X, but painted black. Fared into the leading edge of the cantilever wing* were eight engines, fitted with gleaming metal propellors. The exhaust manifolds were gathered into two large exhaust pipes, one on each side of the hull, that thickened strangely towards the end, and he guessed why the engines made their curious muffled roar. They were silenced. There was no opening in the all-enclosed cockpit, but a door in the huge black hull stood open, and this he assumed gave access to the pilot's seat. Not a sound came from the machine so he approached still closer; it looked as if the entire crew had gone ashore. They would hardly expect visitors, so there was no reason why anyone should stay aboard, he reasoned, glancing over his shoulder at the spark of light that marked the position of the hut. If they were still there, he might have time to have a peep inside. Such a step would be taking a chance, but it was worth it, he decided. Even if they returned and caught him there, what could they do? As a British subject and a retired officer, he would be quite within his rights in making enquiries.

Having made up his mind, he walked quickly across the narrow strip of sand, waded into two feet or so of water, and stepped through the open door into the hull. It was pitch dark inside, so he groped quickly for his matches, and shielding the flame with his hands, struck one.

The cabin in which he found himself was empty, but it was only a small one and he made for the door in the after end. It opened easily and he caught his

* The main beam in this type of wing is supported at one end only.

breath at the sight that met his gaze. For a distance of about twenty feet, set on either side of a narrow gangway, were rows of gleaming steel rods. He knew what they were at once, for he had seen the bomb racks of a big bomber before, but in this case they were on a scale larger than he had ever imagined. He realized with a shock that the machine was no smuggler, but a bomber, a foreign bomber of huge dimensions.

Another door, a small oval one, faced him at the other end of the gangway. He hurried towards it and turned the handle just as his match went out. He stepped across the threshold and took out another match, but at that moment, either on account of his weight, or because of some movement of the tide, the boat gave a sudden list, and he clutched at the side of the hull to save himself from falling. The box of matches flew out of his hand and rattled across the metal floor. With a muttered exclamation of annoyance he dropped on to his knees, and groped for them; as he did so he heard the door swing to with a sharp click. He at once abandoned the matches and sprang back to the door, running his hand swiftly over the smooth metal for the catch. There appeared to be none, or if there was he could not find it. Presently, to his horror, he realized that in the darkness he had lost his sense of direction, and was by no means sure if the wall over which he was running his hands was the one that held the door.

He groped on the floor again for the matches and grunted with satisfaction as his hand struck the elusive box. He took out a match, and was actually holding it in a position to strike, when the sound of voices came faintly from the other side of the partition. For a moment he stood still, thinking hard; to leave the boat without being seen was now obviously impossible. Should he open the door and declare his presence, or remain where he was in the hope of the crew returning to the hut? Something warned him that discovery in his present position was likely to have unpleasant consequences, but before he could make up his mind a sudden vibration told him that the engines had been started. There was a harsh word of command; the sound of a door being slammed was drowned by the roar of the engines as the throttle was opened, and the machine began to surge through the water.

'It looks as if I'm staying here,' he told himself grimly. No good purpose could be served by revealing himself now, so he squatted on the floor and resigned himself to the inevitable. There was just a chance that when the machine reached its destination, wherever that might be, it would be moored without an examination of the aft cabin being made, in which case he might find an opportunity to slip away unobserved.

The machine was in the air now, but he had no idea of the direction in which it was heading; it might have been north, or it might be south for all he knew, and he had no possible means of ascertaining. Had there been a window in the hull it would have been different, but there was not, so all he could do was to sit on the floor and hope for the best. Unusual and unpleasant thoughts began to pass through his mind. Suppose the machine crashed? 'I must have been a blithering idiot to get myself into this mess,' he mused.

How long he sat in the darkness he did not know,

but it seemed like hours, and it was with intense satisfaction that at last he heard the engines being throttled back and knew by the angle of the floor that they were gliding down. 'I wonder where we are now?' he muttered. Without knowing how long he had been in the air, or the speed of the machine, it was impossible to make even the wildest guess as to how far he had travelled, but he knew he might have arrived at almost any point in Europe. He breathed a sigh of relief as the keel kissed the water with a powerful s-s-swish, and he rose to his feet as the engines were switched off.

Again the sound of voices came from the other side of the partition. A door slammed and there was silence. He waited for a few minutes, and then, shielding the flame with his coat, struck a match, blowing it out again as soon as his eyes found the doorlatch, a tiny knob let into the metal, which accounted for his being unable to find it. Hardly daring to breathe, he opened the door an inch and placed his ear to the opening. Not a sound came from the darkness. Leaving the door open behind him he felt his way along the gangway. The door at the far end was closed, but he found the catch and opened it very gently. The forward cabin was also in darkness, but the hull door through which he had entered was open, so with every nerve tense he crept to the door and peeped out. After the stygian darkness of his recent prison, the starlit world seemed as light as day, and he drank in the fresh air in great gulps.

The machine had come to rest about fifty yards from the shore at just such another place as his point of embarkation, except that at a little distance to right and left towered some fairly high cliffs; but the shore immediately opposite was low, and he could hear the waves lapping on the beach. A tiny spark of light glowed just beyond it, and he could just make out the outlines of a small boat hauled up on the sand.

'This is where I step off,' he muttered, as he lowered himself into the water. To his disgust he could not touch bottom, but there was no help for it, and letting go his hold he struck out in the long but quiet breast stroke for the shore, choosing a diagonal course in order to avoid meeting the crew of the flying boat, should they return before he reached the beach. The water was cold and he quickened his stroke, but he seemed to make little progress, and in spite of his efforts he felt a current carrying him towards the spot where the boat lay. For a few minutes he fought against it, but he felt his strength going, and turning over on his back he allowed himself to be carried towards the beach. He had no desire to meet the pilot who had unknowingly given him a lift, but that was preferable to being drowned.

He was nearly spent when his feet touched the bottom, and gasping like a stranded fish he dragged himself ashore. As he waded through the last few yards of water, the moon floated out from behind a cloud and flooded the beach with radiance. There was a sudden shout from the direction of the light on the shore, and the sound of running footsteps, but he heeded them not, for he was far too exhausted. He could not have run a yard if his life had depended on the effort; there are limits to human endurance, so he sank down to recover his breath as quickly as he could.

From a kneeling position he saw four figures running across the soft sand towards him, and he was still panting and spitting out mouthfuls of sea-water when a hand fell on his shoulder and lifted him to his feet. An idea struck him and he played up to it, staggering and clutching at the man who had lifted him, as if to save himself from falling; as a matter of fact the action was not altogether feigned.

'What do you do here?' said a harsh voice.

Biggles looked at the speaker, wringing the water out of his hair as he did so, and saw a hard, military face with piercing eyes set above a well cut nose. A dark moustache adorned the upper lip, and a well-trimmed pointed beard concealed the chin. The man wore a heavy leather coat over a kind of dark uniform.

'What do you do here?' said the man again, sharply.

'Where am I?' gasped Biggles feebly.

'What you do here, eh?' said the man yet again, glancing at his three companions in turn.

'Do here?' said Biggles weakly. 'What do you usually do when you swim ashore after being shipwrecked? I got carried out to sea in my boat, in the storm, this afternoon. She turned over and I hung on to her, but when I saw the coast I let go and swam for it; she's out there somewhere.' He indicated the expanse of ocean vaguely with a wave of his hand.

'So!'

Biggles looked at his questioner. There was no reason why his story of being shipwrecked should not be believed; the very last thing the German – for such he took him to be – would suspect, was that he himself had brought him to the cove in which the giant flying boat now rode at anchor. Yet clearly the man was in a quandary; the very fact that he, Biggles, had seen the big machine, made it necessary that he should not be allowed to depart and report the matter, either out of simple curiosity or because he was suspicious of its design.

'So!' said the man again, still deliberating. Then, as if suddenly reaching a decision, 'Come with me, my friend,' he said.

Obediently Biggles followed him to a small concrete structure about a hundred yards from the shore, alike in every detail to the one he had recently inspected with Algy. He took heart at the sight, for it seemed to show that he was still in England. The bare room was even lighted in the same way as the other had been, with a candle. Two of the men only entered the room with him; the man with the beard, who seemed to be the leader, and another, in an ordinary suit. The other two disappeared; where they went he did not know.

'Do you mind telling me where I am?' asked Biggles rather curtly. 'I'm wet and I'm cold, and I shall have to find somewhere where I can dry my clothes.'

'Yes, yes,' replied the other, stroking his beard.

Biggles could almost read his thoughts; he was wondering if Biggles had seen the flying boat, and if so, what reasonable excuse he could give for its presence. He decided to take the bull by the horns; to pretend that he had not seen the craft was asking for trouble. 'You're Imperial Airways* pilots, I suppose,' he observed. 'Have you made a forced landing?'

'Ah, you saw my aeroplane?' replied the other quickly.

'Of course. I couldn't see much of it because it was too dark, but I thought it was an aeroplane on the water. I've always wanted to fly,' he went on, warming

* The forerunner of British Airways.

33

up to his story. 'Do you think you could give me a joyride sometime?' Biggles was now acting up to the ignorance of the general public where aviation is concerned.

One of the two members of the crew who had disappeared now came to the door and beckoned the leader. Blackbeard, as Biggles mentally styled him, went outside, but returned in a moment or two.

'About this joyride,' he said, looking Biggles straight in the eyes, 'you've never been in an aeroplane perhaps?'

'Never,' lied Biggles unblushingly; the position was far too desperate for squeamishness.

Now there is an old saying that 'truth will out,' and never was it more startlingly demonstrated than at this moment.

'What is your name, by the way?' asked Blackbeard with a curious smile.

'Bigglesworth – James Bigglesworth.'

'I seem to have heard that name before – somewhere. Do you happen to have lost anything?'

Biggles felt quickly in his pockets, and then suddenly understood the meaning of the other's question.

'Is this what you're looking for?' asked Blackbeard, suavely, passing a silver cigarette case.

Biggles stared at it as if it fascinated him – as indeed it did. Somehow it must have slipped out of his pocket while he was on the floor of the cabin groping for the matches. He knew that the men had returned to the flying boat and found it there. Engraved on the front of it were the letters, J. B., and underneath, rather smaller, 'R. F. C.'* If any further proof of his identity was needed, it was there. Inside the case was a photograph of himself, in flying cap, and goggles, standing beside the Vandal. Smyth, his mechanic, had taken it a few days before, and had given him a print just as they were taking off; he had slipped it into his cigarette case for safety. Blackbeard, of course, had seen it; there was no doubt of that. He glanced up and met his mocking eyes.

'I'll give you a joyride,' said the German softly, 'a long one.'

Biggles knew that escape was a matter of now or never, and he acted with the speed of light. He hurled the cigarette case at the candle and sent it spinning; instantly the room was plunged in darkness. A revolver blazed, a streak of fire in blackness, towards the place where he had been standing, but he was no longer there. Simultaneously with his shot at the candle, he had dived for the floor in the direction of the door. He grunted as a heavy boot struck the side of his head, but the owner of it tripped and crashed to the ground, dragging one of the others with him. With a terrific uproar in his ears he reached the door and sped like a deer across the open moor that opened up before him. Again the revolver barked and he heard the shot whistle over his head. Crouching low, he ran on, not knowing in the least where he was, but determined to put as great a distance as possible between himself and the hut. The action restored life to his chilled limbs, and after running about a quarter of a mile he felt that he was clear. He was just about to slow up when his foot caught in an

* Royal Flying Corps, the precursor of the RAF.

unseen obstruction and he crashed heavily to earth. For a moment he lay still, almost stunned by the fall, and then, as he scrambled to his feet a sharp cry of pain escaped his lips. His right ankle refused to support his weight and he sank to the ground again, perspiration breaking out on his face. That he had sprained his ankle, if, indeed, he had not broken it, was certain, and further flight was out of the question. He began to crawl, which was all he could do, looking to right and left for some sort of cover in which to hide. Once or twice he heard his pursuers calling to each other, but they seemed to be some distance away.

Presently he came to a sunken road, or rather, track, and to his almost overwhelming relief, saw a feeble light shining by the side of it not very far away. Between hopping and. crawling, clenching his teeth to stifle the groans of pain that his injured ankle wrung from him, he reached it, and saw that it oozed through a chink in the wall of a sleeper-built railway hut that stood beside a narrow gauge railway, long disused by its overgrown condition, which cut across the sunken road at that point.

'Hullo there!' cried a shrill treble voice from inside. 'Don't stop to knock.'

The humour of the fact that there was no door on which to knock might have made Biggles smile in normal circumstances, but at the moment it was lost on him. He dropped on to his knees, and crawling through the low doorway, found himself staring into the wide open eyes of a lad of fifteen or sixteen years of age. He was in rags, dirty beyond description, but above a collarless shirt rose a frank, alert, freckled face, surmounted by a mop of tousled red hair. The light came from a small fire of sticks, on which rested a small flat tin containing an unpleasant-looking mixture, impossible to describe, but from which arose to Biggles's starved nostrils an appetizing aroma.

'Put that fire out, Ginger – quick!' gasped Biggles.

'What is it – cops after you?' grunted the boy, carefully removing the tin before trampling the fire into extinction. 'Say! If you've broken out of jail you can count on me,' came the small voice from the darkness.

In spite of the pain he was suffering Biggles smiled. 'You've been going to the films, I can see'*, he said. 'Just slip to the door and listen, will you, and tell me if you hear anyone.' He heard the boy cross the hut.

'Nix,' came his voice from the direction of the door.

'Good. Now tell me, what county is this?'

'County? Crumbs, are you so lost that you don't even know what county you're in? You must be lost and no mistake. Fancy not knowing what county you're in.'

'Well come on, what is it?' asked Biggles shortly.

'Well – er – you see – er, now you mention it, I'm not quite sure,' confessed the lad. 'You see,' he went on quickly, 'it's really all the same to me.'

'What was the last big town you saw?'

'Newcastle.'

'How far away is that?'

'Ten miles; fifteen perhaps; maybe twenty. Let's see, I was there two days ago. Must be twenty miles I should say.'

---

* A lot of words Ginger uses such as 'cops' and 'jail' are American terms and were not commonly used in Britain in the 1930s, when this book was written – hence Biggles' comment.

'What the dickens are you doing here?'

'I'm on my way to London.'

'How?'

'Walking – how do you think. You didn't see my Rolls-Royce standing outside as you came in, did you?'

'What are you going to London for?'

'Join the Air Force. If they won't have me, I'm going to Croydon* to watch the air liners. What are you doing here, and how did you get that dud foot? I thought I heard shots just now – was that anything to do with you?'

'It certainly was.'

'Crikey, don't tell me some gang has put you on the spot!'

'They have, or something very much like it. There's a bunch of foreigners on my trail; if they find me, that'll be the end of it.'

'Hey, that's fine. This is the first adventure I've struck since I left Smettleworth.'

'Smettleworth! Where's that?'

'I don't know except that it's the place where I come from. My father's a miner; he fetched me a clip on the ear when I told him I was going to be a pilot, so I hopped it.'

'I see. Well, go and have another listen and then let's sample that fry you've got in the pan.'

'I don't think it's quite done.'

'What is it?'

'Mixed allsorts – bits I scrounged on the way; bread, dripping, potato, turnip, an egg – and things like that.'

* Croydon was used as one of the principal London airports by commercial airlines before the second world war.

'Who gave you the egg?'

'No one – I – er – found it.'

'In somebody's hen house, eh?'

'Never mind that. If you're squeamish I'm not asking you to eat it, am I?'

'How do we eat it?'

'I've got a fork and a spoon and a pocket knife; you can have which you like. I can manage without any of 'em if it comes to that.'

While they had been talking Biggles had taken off his boot and felt his ankle; with the restraining leather removed it was beginning to swell, quickly. 'Just make sure there's nobody about, will you,' he said, 'while I tie up my ankle. I've sprained it.'

'All OK,' said the boy a moment later, after a thorough survey.

'Righto. Then I think you might light the fire again so that I can see what I'm doing. Find some grass, anything'll do, to bung up those chinks where the light gets through. Have you got plenty of sticks?'

'There's a fence outside which should last us; this used to be a level crossing.'

'Fine. Then go and get a good supply, will you? I shall have to try and get my things dry, I'm wet through.' He bound up his foot with his handkerchief and a part of his shirt, and after a frugal but tasty meal, felt considerably better. 'Now, Ginger,' he said, 'I want you to help me.'

'All right, but not so much of the Ginger; my name's Hebblethwaite.'

'Let's stick to Ginger, it's shorter,' suggested Biggles.

'OK with me,' agreed the boy. 'What's your name by the way?'

'Bigglesworth.'

Ginger started violently. 'Bigglesworth! Not the war pilot by any chance?*'

'Well, I was in the War,' confessed Biggles.

'Well strike me pink,' gasped Ginger. 'Biggles in the flesh! This is my lucky day and no mistake; I know all about you so you needn't tell me any more.'

'Oh, and how do you know that?'

'Read about you, of course. You've got a pal named Algy something or other, haven't you? Where's he?'

'I left him with my aeroplane, and I'm afraid he must be getting pretty worried by this time – but never mind that now. This is serious, Ginger, understand that. I meant it when I told you that a gang of crooks are after me. They caught me, but I got away, but this sprained ankle is going to make things awkward. I expect they are still looking for me. You can help me, but you'll have to use your head.'

'OK, chief, just tell me what you want me to do.'

'Is there a town or village anywhere handy?'

'There's a fair sized village about six miles away; I came through it on my way. I don't know the name of it but I'll soon find out.'

'That doesn't matter; what I want you to do is this.' Biggles took out his notebook, removed several water soaked one pound notes, and held them by the fire to dry. 'Take this money,' he went on, 'and find a garage. Get the driver to drive you here as fast as he can to pick me up; you'll probably have to pay him in advance.'

Ginger nodded. 'I get you,' he said.

'Right! Then that's that. I'll get the driver to take me back to the village and then all I shall have to do

---

* See *Biggles in France* and *Biggles Flies East* (published by Red Fox).

is to send a telegram to Algy Lacey at Brooklands Aerodrome. He'll fly up and fetch me.'

'D'you want me to start right away?'

'I'd like you to. You'll find everything shut, of course, at this time of night, but knock up the first garage you come to. If the fellow argues, tell him that there has been an accident and that I'll pay him well for his trouble. Let him see you have money with you. If you can manage to do that, maybe I can give you a lift to London in my machine.'

Ginger's eyes sparkled and he drew a deep breath. 'I'll be back,' he said emphatically, picking up his cap. He thrust the notes deep into his pocket and crossed to the door. 'I'll be seeing you,' he said, and stepped out into the night. For a moment he paused to listen, but hearing nothing set off at a brisk pace along the track. He had gone about half a mile when the beam of a flashlight cut through the darkness from a spot not six yards away; two figures loomed menacingly.

'Why it's a kid,' said one in tones of disgust.

'Say, what's the big idea?' demanded Ginger belligerently; 'you can't go about making people jump that way.' He could just make out the silhouette of a car standing close against the hedge.

'Where have you come from?' asked one of the men gruffly.

Ginger jerked his thumb down the lane. 'There's only one road as far as I can see.'

'You keep a civil tongue in your head, you saucy young pup. Did you see anyone along there?'

'No, worse luck. I was hoping to get a lift. Which way are you going?'

'Mind your own business. We're looking for a

fellow; if you happen to see anyone along the road let out a yell, and I'll give you half a crown*.'

'OK,' replied Ginger briskly, 'if I see him I'll let you know. So long.'

As soon as he was out of earshot he paused to listen. Despite his casual answers, his heart was beating violently, for he had no doubt as to the reason for the men's presence. They were watching for Biggles; should he return and warn him? No, he decided; he might defeat his own object by leading them to his hiding place. He thought swiftly, then hurried on his way. A quarter of a mile farther on he stopped, and cupping his hands round his mouth, let out a piercing yell. He grinned as he heard the engine of the car start up, and climbed up the bank to the edge of the moor. 'This way!' he yelled. 'Here he is,' and crouching low ran out into the darkness. He waited until he heard the car stop, and heavy footsteps thumping in his tracks, and then he gave tongue again. 'Make haste, he's running!' he shouted, and then, silently, and with the stealth of an Indian, began to circle back towards the car. When he reached it he could hear the men muttering in low tones some little distance away, evidently at a loss. He groped in his trousers pocket, produced a jack knife, which he opened, and then felt along the car until his hand reached a tyre. He placed the point of the knife on it and drove it in with all his strength. The tyre was harder than he expected it to be, but the point went home, although to his surprise it made no noise. He could hear the men returning so he jerked out the knife, and the fierce hiss of escaping air that

* In today's currency, 12.5 pence.

accompanied the movement threw him into a panic, for he knew that the men could not have failed to hear it. He heard one of them curse as they started to run back.

Ginger did not wait. With the knife still clasped in his hand he sped down the road like a hare with hounds on its trail, nor did he pause until he was absolutely winded. Then he replaced the knife in his pocket and set off at a steadier pace towards the now visible lights of the sleeping village. A policeman looked at him suspiciously as he struck the first row of houses, and he hesitated, turning over in his mind the advisability of asking the constable to come back with him in the car in case of trouble; but Biggles, he reflected, had said nothing about bringing a policeman, so he dismissed the idea and passed on. He came upon a garage almost at once, easily recognized by an illuminated petrol pump. The place was closed and in darkness, so without the slightest hesitation he beat upon the door with his fist.

A bedroom window was flung open and a man's head appeared. 'What is it?' he asked.

'Have you got a car on hire?' said Ginger.

'Not at this time of night,' was the short reply.

'Never mind the time of night, have you got a car?'

'I have; who wants it?'

'I do.'

'Want me to drive you back to your mansion, eh?'

'My money is as good as anybody else's, isn't it?'

'How much have you got?'

'What's that got to do with you. How much do you charge to drive six miles?'

'Cost you two pounds at this time of night.'

'That's OK. Make it snappy and I'll give you an extra ten bob.'

'What's going on?' asked the man suspiciously, when, a quarter of an hour later, he appeared at the door.

'A gentleman's had an accident down the road and wants you to fetch him.'

'Why didn't you say so before; where's that money?'

'Here you are.'

The man took the two pounds that Ginger gave him, and then dragged back the door of the garage to reappear a moment later with an ancient Ford. 'Get in,' he said. 'Which way?'

'Straight ahead,' replied Ginger. 'Keep going and I'll guide you.'

In twenty minutes they had reached the entrance of the sunken road. 'Go slow now,' Ginger warned the driver, 'but if anyone shoots at us, step on it.'

'Eh! What's that? Did you say *shoot*?'

'Aye. I thought I'd better warn you. If anyone tries to stop us go right ahead.'

'Where do you think we are, in Mexico?' scoffed the driver.

But Ginger wasn't listening; he was looking for the damaged car, but it had gone. 'Whoa!' he cried, when they reached the disused level crossing; 'here we are.' He sprang down as the car pulled up and darted towards the hut. 'Hi! Biggles! we're here!' he cried triumphantly.

There was no reply.

With a curious prickling sensation of the skin he entered the hut and struck a match. It was empty. For a moment he could not believe it. 'Biggles,' he whispered foolishly, 'where are you?' He ran outside, 'Biggles!' he cried loudly, 'Hi, it's me, Ginger.'

Silence.

He stared at the driver of the car white-faced.

'They've got him,' he muttered hoarsely. Then, lifting up his voice, 'Biggles!' he yelled again.

For a minute or two he stood staring into the surrounding darkness. 'Now what are we going to do?' he asked the driver helplessly.

'I don't know what you're going to do, but I'm going home. If I thought you'd brought me out here on a fool's errand—'

'You've been paid, haven't you?' snapped Ginger, 'so what have you got to grouse about. Hold hard a minute, I'm coming with you; it's not much use staying here.'

He left the garage man at his house, giving him the extra ten shillings as he had promised, and made his way, miserable, but deep in thought, further into the village. Again he was tempted to consult a policeman, but could not bring himself to do so. He doubted very much if the police would believe him, anyway, and he could hardly blame them if they did refuse to accept such an improbable story as the one he had to tell. He wandered about until dawn, and then made his way towards the post office.

Chapter 3
A Reconnaissance Flight

Algy landed at Brooklands late in the morning with his mind in a greater turmoil than he could ever remember; he was upset and alarmed, yet he could not bring himself to believe that any tragic fate had overtaken Biggles. Nevertheless, for the first time in his life, he was absolutely at a loss to know what to do for the best, although obviously his first duty would have to be to report the matter to the police.

He left the Vandal on the tarmac for the mechanics to put away, and walked absent-mindedly towards the clubhouse.

'There's a telegram for you, Lacey,' called Benton, a club instructor; who came out of the office as he passed.

'Telegram for me?' cried Algy in amazement. 'Who on earth—' He took the buff envelope down from the rack and tore it open impatiently. It was addressed, simply, Algy Lacey, Brooklands Aerodrome.

'Come at once, bring machine, Biggles captured. Waiting for you at Cramlington Aerodrome.

Ginger.'

Algy read and re-read the wire half a dozen times, trying to grasp its significance; one word only meant anything to him, and that was Biggles. Who Ginger was he had not the remotest idea, or why he was waiting at Cramlington Aerodrome, which is near Newcastle-on-Tyne, yet the word Biggles was enough, and he tore back to the Vandal, startling the mechanics with his impatient demands for the machine to be refuelled. He left a message for Smyth, their mechanic, to stand by in case he was wanted, and within ten minutes was off, and with a slight following wind, touched his wheels on Cramlington Aerodrome in just under two and a half hours. He taxied in and stared about him curiously.

A few yards away a tired-looking boy with sandy hair and a freckled face was coming towards him, regarding him with frank interest, but Algy took no notice; he was accustomed to the curious stares of small boys.

'Are you Algy?' asked a voice apologetically.

Algy stared, and looked at the boy in amazement: 'Some people call me that – why?' he asked.

'I'm Ginger.'

Algy blinked and stared incredulously. 'You mean – you sent me the telegram?'

'Yes, sir, I couldn't think of anything else to do. I'm afraid the gang's got Biggles – I mean Major Bigglesworth.'

'Gang – got him – what gang? What do you know about this. You'd better come over here and tell me all about it.'

Briefly, keeping to the point, yet omitting nothing, Ginger described Biggles' arrival at his bivouac, soaked to the skin, and the subsequent events up to the moment when he had returned with the car only to find that Biggles had disappeared. 'And then,' he concluded, 'I went to the post office and sent that telegram. I wasn't sure where to tell you to come, but

I knew I wasn't far away from Newcastle and I knew Cramlington was the nearest aerodrome to Newcastle. I had some of Big – er – Major Bigglesworth's money left, so I was able to get here. I've got the rest of the money here – you'd better take it.'

'Never mind about that now,' replied Algy shortly, and for a long time sat staring at the ground, deep in thought. 'Do you think you could recognize that place – the hut I mean – if you saw it, from the air?' he asked Ginger at last.

'Well, I've never been up so I don't know, but I'll have a shot at it,' answered Ginger frankly.

'Come on then, let's have a shot at it,' returned Algy. He was now able to form a vague idea of what had happened after Biggles had left him to inspect the mysterious flying boat. As he worked it out, Biggles must have been caught by the crew and taken aboard; it landed again farther on and in some way he had effected his escape. Then he had met Ginger, but had been recaptured while the boy was fetching the car. If that was so, then there was a good reason to suppose that he had been once more taken on board and flown away. In that case, the task of finding him within a radius of nearly two thousand miles, which was probably the machine's endurance range, was hopeless. On the other hand, the presence of the two men with the car, who had intercepted Ginger, suggested that the crew of the flying boat had confederates ashore, as they had in Norfolk. In that case it was not unreasonable to suppose that the flying boat had departed before Biggles had been retaken. He was sure it would try to reach its base, wherever that might be, before dawn. If the flying boat *had* left, then Biggles' captors would take him to their own headquarters, which would certainly be within striking distance of the place where the boat had landed. Moreover, the fact that such a short time had elapsed between Ginger's departure for the car, and his return, added weight to the supposition that the head-quarters, or place from which the people on shore operated, was not far distant from the sea. The first thing to do then, he decided, was to survey the area from the air, and draw such conclusions as were possible.

Ginger literally trembled with excitement when Algy made him sit next to him in the seat which he himself usually occupied when Biggles was flying the machine, but nevertheless, Algy was more than a little shaken by the boy's familiarity with the aeroplane and its component parts. 'How do you know all this?' he asked, as he wound the self-starter.

'Read about it,' Ginger told him. 'I read everything about flying that I can lay my hands on.'

'Well, I must say you haven't wasted your time,' admitted Algy. 'Now listen. I'm going to fly over the district where you were last night; as soon as you spot that railway hut, touch me on the arm and point to it. Got that?'

'OK,' replied Ginger, gazing around with intense satisfaction as the Vandal soared into the air.

Algy headed east and soon struck the coast. For the most part it was rugged, with no possible landing place for a marine aircraft, except at one place, towards which he guided the machine. A flicker of understanding passed over his face as he spotted the concrete hut, identical with the one on the Norfolk coast. 'So that's it, is it,' he mused as he throttled back and dropped down to a thousand feet, eyes probing every yard of the landscape in turn. He picked out the straight track of the narrow gauge railway, and pointed it out to Ginger, who was gazing down with a rapt expression on his face.

'That's it!' shouted Ginger excitedly, pointing with outstretched finger at a small, black, square at the junction of the sunken road and railway.

Algy nodded, and making the hut his centre, began circling in ever widening circles, making a mental note of every building which might be used as a base by the people acting in conjunction with the flying boat. Fortunately there were very few. There were some obviously disused buildings near an old mine-head, a pair of brand new red brick labourers' cottages, a solitary tavern, and one or two isolated farm houses. One house in particular engaged his attention, the nearest one to the creek; it stood some distance back from the road and was almost hidden by a thick growth of ivy. To the north and east it was protected by a clump of wind-twisted fir trees; on the eastern side was a sparse orchard and some ramshackle outbuildings; to the south, an overgrown drive wound through an avenue of trees to the road. 'An ugly place,' he thought, 'anything could happen there.' He jotted down a few notes on his writing pad and made a quick sketch of the district, noting the positions of all the buildings in sight, and was about to turn away when something caught his eye. It was a common enough sight, an ordinary motor car, but it was standing between two of the outbuildings of the ivy-covered house. Remembering what Ginger had told him about the punctured tyre he was tempted to fly low to make a closer examination, but decided it was too risky. If Biggles' abductors were there, he reasoned, they could hardly fail to be perturbed, after what had occurred, by a low-flying aeroplane. From the air he obtained a very good idea of the lay-out of the countryside, and the environs of the ivy-covered house; then, feeling that he could do no more, he returned to the aerodrome.

On the ground, he slowly removed his flying kit, and regarded Ginger thoughtfully. 'What are you going to do now,' he asked.

'What are you?' was the naïve reply. It came so pat that Algy was forced to smile, although he was in no mood for humour.

'Me? Oh, I've got to set about finding Major Bigglesworth,' he said seriously.

'Well, can't I help?'

Algy blinked. 'I don't know,' he said slowly. 'I forgot to thank you for sending me that telegram; you certainly used your initiative there, I must confess. I may need help, and you might be useful. Where were you going when you met Major Bigglesworth?'

'To London; to join the R.A.F.'

Algy raised his eyebrows. 'So ho,' he said, 'a budding airman, eh?'

'I've been in bud for so long, that it's getting time I burst into flower,' Ginger told him quickly. 'I know all about an aeroplane – except how to fly it.'

'I see,' said Algy. 'Well, look here, my lad, you can't go about like that.'

'Like what?'

'In those rags.'

Ginger flushed. 'They're the best I've got,' he observed.

'That's what I mean. Here's some money; add that to the change you've got left out of Major

51

Bigglesworth's money. Slip into Newcastle and get yourself a serviceable outfit and then come back here; I'm going to do a bit of scouting tonight.'

'You mean, round the house where the car was?'

Algy opened his eyes wide. 'So you spotted that, did you?' he asked.

'Of course, I was on the lookout for a car; d'you think that's where they've got Biggles?'

'It struck me as being the most likely place.'

'What are you going to do, go to the police?'

'I suppose I should really, but they might mess the whole thing up. In the first place I should probably have a job to make them believe me, and secondly, while they were pottering about getting search warrants and so on, anything could happen. I feel inclined to have a prowl round myself first; if the job proves too big to handle I shall have to call in the police. But that's enough for the present; you get off to Newcastle for some clothes and some food and then come back. I'll get a car, one that I can drive myself, and we'll have a look round tonight.'

'OK, I'll be seeing you.'

Algy watched the little upright figure disappear briskly round the corner, with a peculiar smile on his face. 'I like the way that kid walks and the way he holds his head up,' he mused, as he made his way towards the club house.

Chapter 4
In The Enemy Camp

Biggles, after Ginger had departed to fetch the car, made himself as comfortable as possible by the small fire, and prepared to wait. He was well aware that by keeping the fire alight he was taking a big risk of being found, but he had no alternative without running the risk of getting double pneumonia by sitting in soaking wet clothes for a couple of hours or more. However, he hoped that his pursuers had given up the chase. Once, shortly after Ginger's departure, he thought he heard a shout in the distance, but he was not sure. What he heard was Ginger's shout to lead the men with the car off the trail, but of course he was not to know that. With the lad out of the way he was able to arrange his coat and trousers, boots and socks, completely round the fire, while he himself crouched over it as near as he could get without actually burning himself. An hour passed slowly and he felt certain that Blackbeard and company had abandoned their search for him, so he threw the rest of the wood on to the fire, and soon had his clothes dry enough to put on. The fire died down to a heap of glowing embers, and although his twisted ankle was still giving him a good deal of pain, he dropped off into a doze.

He was awakened by a low growl from the open doorway, and looking up with a start, could just make out the head of a large animal, its eyes reflecting the glow of the embers. He knew at once that it could only be a dog, so he did the best thing he could in the circumstances; he spoke to the animal in a quiet, caressing voice, hoping to put it at its ease. 'What's the matter, old man?' he said coaxingly, but nevertheless ran his eye over the floor for a weapon in case the beast proved savage. The only answer he got was another growl, and as the dog came farther into the hut, he saw that it was a large, black Alsatian, a breed that has too much of the wolf in it to be either courageous or reliable. It growled again and showed its fangs wickedly. 'All right, have it that way if you like; get out, you brute,' snapped Biggles.

Instantly there was a shout outside. 'Come on, here he is,' cried a voice. There was a low whistle, which the dog quickly obeyed, and disappeared; heavy footsteps sounded just outside the open doorway.

'Come on out of that,' said a voice.

Biggles stiffened, but made no reply. Had there been a door, he would have tried to hold the place until Ginger's return, trusting that he brought a driver who would stand by him; but as there was no door and he had no weapon, he was helpless.

'Did you hear what I said – outside!' repeated the voice venomously.

Still Biggles made no reply. The muzzle of an automatic appeared in the doorway, slowly followed by a hand and arm, and then a face; Biggles recognized the man at once for one of those he had seen in the hut with Blackbeard.

'Yes, what do you want?' he asked coldly.

'I'll show you presently,' replied the man, and then, to someone outside, 'Serge, slip up and fetch the car; never mind that tyre, get it along somehow. And you sit still till you're told to move,' he went on, nodding evilly at Biggles. 'The Boss wants a word with you.'

In two or three minutes the car came chugging down the road, with its driver cursing the faulty steering caused by the punctured tyre.

'Come on, get in,' said the man at the door. 'You can either come on your feet or be knocked on the head and carried. If I had my way I should know how to deal with you.'

'Are you an Englishman?' asked Biggles curiously.

'I was – till I did ten years at Dartmoor*.'

'Well, I expect you deserved it; you'll do another ten shortly or I'm very much mistaken,' said Biggles, rising with difficulty and putting on his coat. Resistance was useless; he had no desire to add another injury to his damaged ankle, which was giving him quite enough trouble.

'Stow that gab; step out and look lively.' The man thrust the automatic roughly into Biggles' side as he limped out of the doorway. 'You do what you're told – see,' he snarled.

Biggles climbed into the back seat of the car, and the man got up beside him. 'Off you go, Serge,' he told the driver.

The jolting of the damaged car up the rough road caused Biggles excruciating agony, and he was glad when it reached the main road. Presently it turned off down a lane, or drive, and pulled up in front of a fairly large house. He was dragged roughly out of the car and hurried up two flights of stairs into a room; the door slammed behind him and he was left alone.

---

* High security prison located on the isolated moorland of Dartmoor, Devon.

There was no artificial light, but sufficient starlight to see that the room was roughly furnished as a bedroom. He crossed at once to the window, but two iron bars had been screwed vertically over it, evidently in anticipation of his capture, and as far as he could make out from his limited field of view, a sheer drop of twenty or thirty feet into a courtyard lay below it. Escape, that way, particularly in his present lame condition, was out of the question, and he quickly made up his mind that all he could do was to wait for daylight to get a better idea of his position.

There were no blankets on the bed and he passed a miserable night, or such as was left of it, but when dawn came he was glad to see that the swelling of his ankle had abated slightly. He rebound it firmly, using strips of his shirt for the purpose, which brought relief. At about eight o'clock, the man with whom he had previously spoken, brought him a jug of tea and some bread and butter, and departed without a word.

Biggles was thankful for the food, for he was almost famished, and after eating it was about to make another survey of his prison, when the sound of a car outside took him to the window, which he now saw overlooked some outbuildings and a grass-grown drive, up which a powerful car was approaching. He watched it curiously until it swung out of sight round a corner of the house, where he heard it stop. Almost immediately afterwards, heavy footsteps sounded on the uncarpeted stairs and the key of his room rattled in the lock.

The door was pushed open and three men entered; one, who treated the others with deference, was the man who had been responsible for Biggles' capture; the other two were strangers, and that they were both foreigners was obvious at a glance. One, who seemed to be the senior, was an elderly, stoutly-built man with a grey beard, high cheekbones, and piercing eyes. He wore a dark overcoat with an astrakhan collar. The other was lean, swarthy, with black hair and a drooping black moustache; his expression was cold and cruel, and he instantly reminded Biggles of someone he had seen on the films, a professional killer in a gangster picture.

The elderly man sat on the edge of the bed and regarded Biggles for some moments without speaking. Then, rising to his feet and facing him squarely, he said, slowly and deliberately, 'What were you doing in that aeroplane?'

'Whatever I was doing does not authorize you to take the law into your own hands,' Biggles told him shortly.

'Answer my question.'

'What do you suppose I was doing – trying to get a free flight? That I was on it in the creek where your fellows found me I'll not deny, but it was by accident. It was either that or be drowned. My one idea was to get off it as quickly as possible, as you must realize if you have all the facts before you; otherwise, why should I be such a fool as to come ashore as I did?'

'Where did you board it?'

'On the water of course, where else? Don't ask me to name the place because I can't. I suspect we are in Northumberland, but I am by no means sure.' Biggles spoke the literal truth, and said the words with conviction.

His interrogator changed the subject. 'Your name is Bigglesworth, is it not?'

'It is.'

'Not by any chance the Major Bigglesworth who acquired a reputation during the War?'

'I served during the War, if that is what you mean, and, I hope, not entirely without success.'

The man exchanged glances with his companions and nodded slowly. 'And now you are in the British Intelligence Service, eh?' he asked quietly.

Biggles laughed; he could not help it. 'I am not,' he said. 'I have been abroad until recently*, but at present I am doing nothing. I am not in any way connected with any branch of either the intelligence or regular services.'

'Do you expect us to believe it was by accident that you were on our flying boat last night?'

'I do not, it sounds much too unlikely,' admitted Biggles, 'but I can only assure you that at this time yesterday I had not the remotest idea that such a craft existed.'

'But unfortunately for yourself you know now.'

'Why unfortunately? From what I saw of it it was an extremely interesting-looking machine, and I should like to see more of it.' Biggles spoke lightly, but he did not deceive himself as to the other's meaning.

'Perhaps you will, my young friend, perhaps you will,' the man assured him. 'You may see more of it than you wish.'

'May I inquire the purpose of this conversation, and how much longer you propose to continue this outrage?' asked Biggles coldly.

'The answer to the first part of your question is that I wished to satisfy myself as to your identity, and possibly ascertain why you were so ill-advised to meddle

* See *Biggles: The Cruise of the Condor* (published by Red Fox).

in matters that do not concern you. The answer to the second I cannot for the moment furnish. I am very much afraid I shall have to take you for a long flight, Major Bigglesworth. You are not by any chance seeking employment?'

'Not with you.'

'And it would be too much to expect you to give your word of honour that if I released you, you would forget the existence of the flying boat and what you have seen?'

'You are quite right, it would.'

'Ah! I was afraid so. In that case your fate is in your own hands; you will return as a passenger in the machine the next time she visits this coast. After that—' The man shrugged his shoulders, and followed by the others left the room without another word. Presently Biggles saw the car departing down the drive.

'This is a bigger thing than I imagined,' he soliloquized, 'and that fellow, I fancy, is the boss. They must have got in touch with him at once after last night's affair, and he made a special journey to see me. Well, I should like to know where his headquarters are. I wonder what the dickens poor old Algy is thinking by this time.'

As if in answer, the low drone of an aeroplane engine reached his ears; at first he paid little attention to it, thinking it was some club machine on a cross-country flight, or joyride, but when the deep bellow of the Napier Lion became recognizable he jumped to the window, and stared up eagerly. It was the Vandal!

To say that he was surprised would be to put it mildly, and for the moment he could not imagine how on earth Algy had learned where he was. He had taken it for granted that Ginger, on returning to the hut and finding he had disappeared, would proceed on his way to London, the richer for the change out of the money he had given him. 'Ginger must have got in touch with him somehow or other; there's no other possible solution,' he mused. 'Good for him. I mentioned Brooklands now I come to think of it; he must have fetched Algy up here. Smart lad, that.'

The arrival of Algy on the scene put a different complexion on matters, although on further consideration, it was hard to see how he could help him. Had he been able to signal to the machine, still circling above, something might be done to effect his rescue, but as it was there was no way of letting them know just where he was. Algy could hardly be expected to know the actual house in which he was confined, and there would certainly be other houses about, he reflected. He was glad to see the machine however, for its presence was a link with Algy, and he was half sorry when it presently drifted out of sight and the noise of the engine faded into silence.

A frugal lunch was brought in about one o'clock by the same man who had brought his breakfast.

'When's the flying boat coming over here again?' Biggles asked him as he was about to leave the room without speaking.

'It'll be soon enough for you,' the man assured him truculently.

'What a nice cheerful cove you are,' muttered Biggles as the fellow went out and slammed the door behind him.

The afternoon passed slowly, and as the daylight began to fade he grew irritated at his enforced inaction. 'I shall go crazy if they keep me here long, doing nothing,' he growled, and examined the room for the hundredth time. Every article that might have been used as an instrument to prise open or break down the door or window, had been removed. The door admittedly did not look very strong, being of an ordinary, cheap sort, but it refused to give in the slightest degree to the pressure of his shoulder, and as he knew that more forcible methods could not be employed without a good deal of noise, he turned again to the window.

It was now nearly dark, but a slight movement caught his eye, a movement that from his elevated position was quite plain, but which would be invisible from the ground floor. He peered forward through the glass and saw a small figure creeping stealthily along the side of the old-fashioned coach house, keeping close to the brickwork. He watched it breathlessly as it reached a corner, straightened, and looked up, eyes roving slowly over the house. As the face turned towards the window through which Biggles was staring, he saw that it was Ginger. The boy saw him at the same moment. He raised his hand to show that he had seen him, and then disappeared. His departure was so swift and unexpected that at first Biggles could not believe that he was no longer there, and he continued to stare at the spot, aware that his heart was beating furiously. He watched the place where Ginger had disappeared until it was quite dark, half expecting some signal to be made, but none came. 'Well, at least they know where I am,' he thought jubilantly.

Chapter 5
Rescue

When Ginger had disappeared, he had merely dropped flat and then wormed his way on his stomach, like a snake, to the rear of the building. On reaching it he glanced quickly to right and left and then darted into an evergreen shrubbery just beyond it. Five minutes later he arose, filthy and begrimed, from a ditch a good hundred yards away from the house. He doubled down a hedge to the road, paused for an instant to listen, and then, crossing it swiftly, made his way down the hedge on the far side, and presently broke into a trot which he kept up until he came to a coppice, nearly a quarter of a mile away. Even there he did not relax his caution, but moved through the trees with no more noise than a shadow, and with unerring instinct struck his object at the first attempt. It was a motor car, parked just inside the coppice which adjoined the road.

Algy was standing by the radiator in a listening attitude, but he started violently as Ginger rose up, out of the ground as it were, by his side. 'Great Scot! You made me jump,' he ejaculated. 'It looks to me as if you were right,' he added, referring to Ginger's insistence that he, not Algy, should take the first scouting expedition from the rendezvous they had established that evening after leaving the aerodrome as arranged. Algy, not unnaturally, had been in favour of leaving Ginger with the car, but Ginger would not hear of it. 'For one thing,' he had said, 'you are twice as big as I am, which means that you stand double the chance of being spotted; and for another, I'm used to this sort of thing and you're not.'

Algy did not ask him how it was that he was 'used to that sort of thing,' but he eyed him suspiciously.

'Well, he's there,' said Ginger casually.

'How do you know?' asked Algy quickly.

'I saw him.'

'Where?'

'At a window; he's right up the top of the house.'

For a moment Algy stared at him; 'You ought to have been an Indian,' he told him.

'I should say I ought,' replied Ginger in his best American drawl. 'Well, I guess we'd better go and get him,' he added.

'I think I ought to go and fetch the police.'

'That's a bright idea. I can see them handling this job; by the time they had got a search warrant and all the rest of it Biggles would be anywhere but in that house. Even now they might shift him at any minute. Pretty fools we should look if we went to the police and then came back and found the place empty.'

'Perhaps you're right.'

'There's no perhaps about it.'

'Well, I'm an amateur at housebreaking so I shall have to go and have a look round before I decide on a plan. We haven't a weapon between us and these fellows are certain to be armed. I wonder how many there are of them?'

'I didn't see anybody except Biggles, but I knew he was there before I saw him.'

'How?'

'I found the car with the burst tyre. I crawled all

round the house, staring at every window, before I spotted him; then I gave him the OK and came back.

'I'd better go and have a look at that window.'

'I shouldn't; you might be spotted. The next time we go up there will be to fetch Biggles. I've got an idea.'

'Well, what is it?'

'The first thing to do is to get the other people out of the house.'

'And how do you propose to do that – go up and ask them if they'd kindly step outside while—'

'Shucks! I could think of a dozen ways to get them out. I'll fetch them out, don't you worry. Now this is my scheme. First of all we cut a couple of good cudgels.'

'I haven't a knife—'

'You ought to carry one. I never move without mine. I was saying, we cut a couple of cudgels and take that spare can of petrol—'

'You're not going to set the place on fire!'

'I didn't say I was; I wish you'd give me a chance to finish. What was I saying? Oh yes, the petrol. Now this is the racket. We go up to the house together. When we get there I'll show you the toolshed where you get an axe; I know there's one there because I've seen it.'

'What's the axe for?'

'For you to beat Biggles's door in with, of course.'

'I see.'

'Then you stand by the back door and wait for the people to run out. They'll run out, you can bet on that. When they run out you run in.'

'But wait a minute, what's going to make them run out?'

'Don't you worry about that, that's my job. I've always wanted to light a good bonfire and this is my chance. That's all there is to it. You watch the door; when they run out, in you go and scoot up to the second floor. When you get there yell for Biggles. He'll answer you and then you'll know which room he's in. Then all you have to do is to bash in the door with the axe and make for the car.'

'Pretty good,' admitted Algy admiringly, 'when did you think of all this?'

'Think of it! I didn't have to think; it just came sort of natural.'

Algy grinned. 'Good enough,' he said, 'let's cut those cudgels.'

In a few minutes they were on their way to the house. It was pitch dark, but Ginger seemed to have the eyes of a cat, and Algy followed him blindly, scratching his hands and face more than once on the brambles of the hedge.

'Don't make such a noise,' whispered Ginger, 'you remind me of an elephant in a jungle.'

'Where did you see an elephant in a jungle, anyway?'

'On the films. Quietly now. Here we are, that's the door you've got to watch; it's the back door and the one they'll come out of. Here's the toolhouse; wait a minute while I fetch the axe.' He was back in a moment and thrust the weapon into Algy's hand.

'Suppose they come out of the front door?' asked Algy.

'They won't. Now you keep under cover or they may spot you in the glare. Watch the fireworks – so long.' With the cudgel in his right hand and the tin of petrol in the other he vanished into the darkness.

As silently as a ghost he made his way through the maze of outhouses until he came to the one he sought; it had once been a stable and the floor was still littered with straw; several trusses of hay were piled in the corner.

He unscrewed the lid of the petrol can easily, for he had given it a start before he left the car, and poured the spirit over the hay. He had stood the tin down on the floor, and was feeling in his pocket for the matches, when a slight sound made him turn. A long, low shadow was creeping towards him, making a deep growling sound as it advanced.

He felt the hair slowly rise on his scalp, and a prickling sensation ran down his spine. Then, as the sinister shadow drew level with the doorway, he saw that it was a huge black Alsatian, that was evidently kept in the stable. He caught his breath sharply, gripped his cudgel with both hands and waited; there was nothing else he could do, for the brute was between him and the door. The dog stopped, and for what seemed an eternity the two faced each other.

'Get out of here,' snapped Ginger.

Then the beast sprang. As the shadow left the floor Ginger leapt sideways, and brought the cudgel down with all his force; he aimed at its head, but struck an even more vulnerable spot, its muzzle. The click of the heavy piece of wood as it smashed on to the bone, made him feel sick, but he had no choice; the wolfish animal would tear him to pieces if it could. With a dreadful noise that was half a howl of pain and half a roar of rage it spun round as it landed on the floor and attacked again, but now keeping a watchful eye on the stick that Ginger whirled in front of him like a flail. Had the dog been a bulldog there could only

66

have been one ending to such an encounter, but the Alsatian lacks the deadly dogged ferocity of its smaller brother. It charged again however, and Ginger was forced to step back; as he did so he trod on a thick object and something struck him a sharp blow on the back of the head. He knew what it was under his foot by the way it 'gave' – the stable broom. He had stepped on the bristles and the stick had flown up and hit him. He could not have wished for a more fortunate circumstance, for a broom with stiff bristles is the best defence in the world against an angry dog, a fact of which he was well aware. He dropped his cudgel and grabbed the broom. The Alsatian, seeing the cudgel fall, snatched at the opportunity and sprang, but the stiff wire-like bristles leapt out to meet him, and caught him fairly across the eyes. With a frightful howl it turned tail and dashed out of the doorway, followed by the broom. Ginger snatched up his cudgel with a trembling hand, for the experience had been an unnerving one, and took out his matches. He leapt like a deer away from the conflagration that seemed to spring towards the match as he struck it, and dashed out of the doorway looking to right and left for the dog; but it had disappeared.

He had barely reached the shelter of a clump of laurels when the back door was flung open and a man emerged.

'I'm sure I heard that dog bark,' he was saying to somebody inside, and then, raising his voice, 'Zulu! Here! Zulu! Here—' His call broke off abruptly as he saw the fire leaping skyward from the stables. 'Look out!' he yelled, 'get some water, the place's on fire.' He was joined by two other men and all three of them rushed into the open, each shouting instructions to the others. 'Get the hose, get the hose!' cried one. 'It's in the toolshed; buckets are no use.'

Ginger, from his place of concealment, saw Algy dart across the lurid glow into the back door; a sound of hammering came from inside the house even above the noise of the devouring flames.

'That fellow upstairs is trying to get out!' shouted one of the men, tugging at a length of garden hose, which was in a hopeless tangle.

'Let him!' screamed one of the others. 'He can't get out; if the house catches fire it'll save us a lot of trouble.' He ran across the courtyard, uncurling the hose as he ran, and cursing like a madman as he tried to straighten it out, came to a stop not a yard from the place where Ginger knelt, watching. By the merest chance he happened to look up just as Algy ran out of the house with Biggles limping beside him. 'Look out!' he yelled, and whipped out an automatic. The range was point blank, and in the glare of the now leaping flames, it was as light as day; to miss such a target as Biggles and Algy presented was almost impossible, for Biggles was unable to move very fast, and they still had seven or eight yards to go before they could reach the cover of the nearest out-buildings.

The man – it was the one who Biggles knew so well – raised his weapon and took deliberate aim.

Ginger sprang to his feet, and taking the end of the cudgel in both hands, brought it round with a terrific swipe straight across the man's shins. Under the force of the blow, the wood, a piece of tough ash, flew to splinters. The man let out a piercing shriek of anguish; the automatic flew out of his grasp and he crashed to the ground, clutching at his injured legs and moaning dreadfully.

At his first yell of agony the other two men had looked toward him, and seeing what was happening added their shouts to the din. Ginger leapt into the open, snatched up the automatic and pointed it towards them. It was no time to utter warnings, he decided, and began pumping out lead as fast as he could pull the trigger. Five rounds he fired before the two men, who had fled before his fusillade, disappeared round a corner of the house. Where his bullets went Ginger did not know, nor did he stop to find out; he dropped the weapon into his pocket and dashed off in the direction taken by Biggles and Algy. Rounding the end of the outbuildings he saw that they were about fifty yards away, Biggles hobbling as fast as he could towards the road with Algy helping him.

A shot rang out from somewhere behind, and Ginger faced round, feeling in his pocket for the automatic. One of the men was close behind him, but he dashed back as Ginger's gun blazed in his face. A piece of brick flew out of the wall not a foot from his head.

'Stay back there!' yelled Ginger, 'or I'll drill you like – like a . . . now what the dickens do they drill people like?' he growled. 'Colander – that's it.' Then, raising his voice, 'I'll drill you guys into a colander – two colanders,' he bellowed. Then, to himself, as he retreated down the drive, 'That doesn't sound right to me; I'll have to look that up in a book.'

'Keep going,' he called to Biggles and Algy, who had turned round to wait for him when they saw him coming. 'Get to the car.'

A bullet whistled over his head, but it was the last one of the action.

'You be careful what you are doing with that gun, my lad,' Biggles told him seriously, as Algy started up the car, and they climbed in. 'You had better give it to me before you hurt yourself; where did you get it?'

'Spoils of war,' replied Ginger, 'I shall need it, too, from what I can see of it, if I am going to see much of you two.'

'Where are we going,' asked Algy from the wheel.

'Anywhere,' replied Biggles. 'Let's get away from here for a start; then we'll make for the nearest town. Where is the machine?'

'Cramlington.'

'Where are we now?'

'About an hour's run from Newcastle.'

'Then make for Newcastle. We'll get rooms there for the night and then tomorrow decide what we are going to do; we shall have a lot to talk about.'

'What I should like to know is, how the dickens did you get up here?' asked Algy, as they sped along the road.

'I'll tell you all about it presently,' replied Biggles. 'What I want is some food, a bath and a general overhaul.'

Chapter 6
Council Of War

Two days later they sat basking in the autumn sun-shine at a quiet spot on the aerodrome at Cramling-ton. Nothing of interest or importance had occurred since the rescue, for which Biggles' sincere thanks had brought a flush of pleasure to Ginger's face. They had compared notes and decided that in the circumstances their obvious and proper course was to report the whole matter to the authorities and leave them to finish the affair with the more efficient resources at their disposal.

Biggles had accordingly drafted out a detailed report, describing the position of the hidden flood-lights, and despatched it to the Intelligence branch of the Air Ministry. Having thus washed their hands of the affair, as they thought, they had discussed Ginger's future, with the result that they had decided to take him back to London with them and endeavour to secure his entry into the Royal Air Force as an aircraft apprentice, failing which they would use their influ-ence to get him a place in one of the many aircraft manufacturing firms they knew, with a view to sub-sequently obtaining his ticket as a ground engineer. Biggles had also agreed, in return for his part in the rescue, to have him taught to fly at a school – a proposal that met with Ginger's entire approval. They were in no immediate hurry to return, so they spent their time between Newcastle and the aerodrome, waiting for Biggles's ankle, which was rapidly mending, to become quite sound again.

Algy had given Ginger several flights in the Vandal and had shown him how to work the controls; on one occasion, to his intense joy, Ginger had even been allowed to hold the joystick for a few minutes while they were in the air.

'It was my lucky day when I fell in with you and no mistake,' he said with an emphasis that made them laugh. Indeed, the lad's strange, but inoffensive air of familiarity and self assurance, combined with his occasional lapses into American film jargon, caused them endless amusement.

'Don't be too sure of that,' Biggles told him seriously, 'we never know quite what is going to happen next – Hullo, this fellow's looking for us I fancy.'

A steward had appeared round a corner of the clubhouse and was pointing them out to two smartly-dressed men, who walked quickly towards them.

'Major Bigglesworth?' asked one as they came up.

'That is my name,' replied Biggles. 'Forgive me for not getting up, but I've had a little trouble with one of my ankles.'

'Certainly. I am Squadron Leader Taglen, of the Air Ministry, and this is Colonel Barlow of the Special Intelligence. You sent in a report recently.'

'I did.'

'Why did you do that?'

'Why?' Biggles opened his eyes wide. 'Because I thought you would be glad to have the information.'

'Was it intended to be a joke?'

Biggles frowned. 'What do you mean?' he asked

tersely. 'It was anything but a joke for us I can assure you.'

Taglen looked at him queerly. 'I cannot think of any other reason why you should send us off on such a wild goose chase. We know your record, of course. You have been an officer, a responsible officer holding a Command. What made you do this, Bigglesworth?'

Biggles stared at him in amazement. 'What the dickens are you driving at?' he replied curtly. 'Are you suggesting that I'm a liar? You can soon satisfy yourself of the truth of the matter by inspecting the places I named in my report. I told you exactly where you would find the switches controlling the floodlight.'

'I know; we've been there.'

'Then why do you take this attitude?'

Taglen looked at Colonel Barlow with an odd expression, then back at Biggles. 'Are you really serious?' he asked.

'Dash it all, man, do you think I'd be likely to invent such a yarn?'

'We thought not, but there is little to substantiate it.'

'But the floodlights?'

'There are no floodlights there – nothing at all.'

Biggles sprang to his feet, his injured ankle forgotten. 'Good God!' he cried, suddenly understanding. 'But you saw the mark on the wall?'

'There is no mark.'

'But the switch under the floor?'

'If there is a switch we were unable to find it.'

Biggles threw up his hands. 'I might have guessed it,' he muttered bitterly. 'But what about that house, though, where I was held prisoner?' he added quickly.

'There is no such house.'

'You mean you couldn't find it?'

'We found where there had been a house.'

'Don't talk in riddles, man, what do you mean?'

'The house has been burnt down; there is only a charred skeleton left.'

Biggles looked at Ginger with a grim smile. 'You either made a bigger bonfire than you intended, my lad – or else they have deliberately burnt the place down to cover up their tracks. Well, Taglen, I am sorry,' he went on, turning to the others, 'but I can only give you my word that everything I told you in that report was true, and to my mind the subsequent actions of these people, the swift and efficient way in which they have removed all traces, goes to show how serious the matter is.'

'Personally, I believe you,' Taglen told him, 'but whether the higher authority will take the same view or not I cannot say. But one thing is certain: there is nothing left for us to work on, not a single clue. If you hear any more about the affair, or pick up the thread again, perhaps you will be good enough to let me know. You can always get in touch with me at the Ministry.'

'I will.'

'That's all there is to be said then; we might as well be getting back. Good morning, Bigglesworth.'

'Well what do you know about that?' asked Biggles, after the two officials had departed. 'By James, these people waste no time; they knew we should have to report the matter as soon as I got away, and acted accordingly. They're smart and no mistake. Well, come on.'

'Where are you going?' asked Algy.

'Norfolk. Before I do anything else I am going to

satisfy myself that what these fellows told us is true. I don't doubt it for an instant, mind you, but – well, I'd just like to have a look around. What are you going to do?' The last remark was addressed to Ginger, who had whipped a flying cap and pair of goggles from his pocket – two presents from Algy.

Ginger's face fell. 'Aren't I coming with you?' he cried despairingly. His disappointment was so genuine that Biggles' heart softened.

'But this is all very fine, my lad,' he said, 'what is your father going to say if anything happens to you? This may turn out to be no joyride you know.'

'Oh there's no need to worry about that,' replied Ginger quickly, 'I wrote a postcard from Newcastle to say I'd got a job, flying.'

'And what did he say to that? Was he pleased?'

'Well – er—' Ginger looked sheepish. 'Not exactly pleased. He said—' He took a dirty envelope from his pocket.

'Just what did he say – come on, let's have the truth.'

'Well, if you must know, he said that if I broke my blinking neck it would be my own fault.'

'And he'll be quite right. Very well, you can come, but you do what you're told – understand?'

Ginger nodded. 'OK, chief,' he said brightly.

They reached the creek on the Norfolk coast about the middle of the afternoon, and after a brief survey of the landscape from the air, landed in exactly the same place as when they had been forced down by the storm. Seen in the clear light of day, its utter solitude was even more depressing than before, for the only signs of life were the wheeling seagulls. They taxied to the beach and walked quickly up to the hut, where a quick examination revealed that what Taglen had told them was true in every detail. Not a sign or mark of any sort remained; the place might have been unvisited since it was abandoned at the end of the War; even the candle had gone, and the mark on the wall had been carefully erased. They dug into the sandy floor, but all they uncovered was more sand.

'Well, that's that,' observed Biggles. 'I don't think it's any use going back to the place on the Northumberland coast, because if they have made such a thorough clean up here, they will certainly have done the same thing there. It looks as if we've come to a dead end.'

'Not quite,' said Algy slowly, 'I've still a card up my sleeve.'

'What's that?' asked Biggles sharply.

'You remember the night you left me here, and I crept up to the hut to see what I could find out?'

'Perfectly well.'

'I risked a peep through the window, and this is what I saw. The head chap – you know, the one with the black beard—'

Biggles nodded.

'He had got a map held up against the wall,' went on Algy. 'I couldn't see very much, but I just had time to spot one or two things. The first was that there were several marks – six or seven I should think – on the east coast of England. We know about two of them; one was the place on which we are now standing, and the other was in Northumberland. If you remember, the sign on the wall had a number over it – a figure eight, in Roman numerals, wasn't it? Well, I should say this place was number eight; there are still six others that we haven't located. I noticed that one seemed to be somewhere in Essex, but I was too far away to see the exact spot. The important thing is though, that from each one of these places, a line had been drawn, in the way they mark shipping routes on a map, to a spot in Europe, which, I imagine, is the headquarters of the whole thing. It looked to me as if a course had been plotted on the map to each one of the places over here.'

'Where was this place?' asked Biggles abruptly.

'I'm not quite certain because it was a small scale map, but I could put my finger on the spot to within fifty or a hundred miles. The lines ran straight across the North Sea, across northern Germany, to the Baltic coast. They either ended in Eastern Prussia, or in Russia. I fancy it was Russia.'

Biggles whistled softly. 'Russia, eh? By James!' he went on quickly, 'You're right. Those fellows who came to see me in the house were Russians; I'd bet on it. I couldn't quite make out what they were at the time; I put them down as Germans, but I was by no means sure of it. One might have been a German, but I'll swear the other was a Russian; he had high cheek bones – a typical Slav.'

'Well, that's where the big machine started from and where it's gone back to,' declared Algy.

'What about—'

'Well?'

'I was just wondering.'

'Yes, and I know what you were wondering. You were thinking about flying over the ditch and having a look round?'

'You've got it,' admitted Biggles. 'It would be a bit risky—'

'I don't see why it should be if our papers are in

77

order. We've got our passports. We can get carnets*
from the Aero Club, and set off on an ordinary air
tour. Who is going to say that we aren't just air
tourists?'

'That might be all right in most places, but I'm not
so sure about Russia**. I do not think we should be
able to get permission to even fly over Russian terri-
torial waters. If we did go without permission, and
had to come down for any reason, there would be the
dickens of a stink. I don't want to end my days in
Siberia. Blackbeard knows us, don't forget that. If he
saw us it wouldn't be much use saying we were just
on a harmless tour.'

'Then why not go to Germany? Let's go as far as
the Baltic and see what happens there before we make
further plans.'

'Yes, we could do that. It looks to me as if both
Russia and Germany are in this; they have got an
understanding, with Great Britain as the mutual
objective. It's a long way from Russia to here, but not
too far for a high efficiency bomber. If they'll go as
far as fitting up elaborate floodlights over here, there
is no reason why they shouldn't have petrol dumps
for refuelling; submarines could lie around the coast

* Touring abroad by air is not merely a matter of 'Go as you please.'
The aircraft must carry a Journey Logbook (which is made up like a
ship's log), an Aircraft Log, Engine Log, and Pilot's Logbook. The
Journey Logbook must be made up at each port of call and signed by
a responsible official. Then there is the Custom's Carnet (pronounced
carnay) which is issued by the Royal Aero Club to avoid difficulties
with customs officials in the matter of import duties. The machine's
Certificate of Airworthiness must be carried; the pilot must carry his
Pilot's Certificate and the Registration Certificate of the aeroplane.
Passports must, of course, be carried, and endorsed or visaed at certain
places. – W. E. J.
** Ex-Soviet Union, now the area known as the Russian Federation.

with petrol and oil on board, if it comes to that. Well, we've nothing else to do; if there is a plot afoot it's up to us to find out what it is, if we can.'

'You've sure spilt a bibful,' observed Ginger. 'I guess—'

'You keep your guesses under your hat for a bit, my lad, and for goodness sake stop that Yankee drawl, or you'll have us all doing it before you've finished.'

'OK baby – sorry – I mean, righto.'

'That's better.'

'That's settled then,' put in Algy.

'Yes, we'll get back to Brooklands and fix things up; it shouldn't take more than a day or two.'

'That's fine,' declared Ginger.

'I didn't say you were coming.'

'I know you didn't, but I sort of took it for granted.'

'You take too much for granted young fellow-me-lad. You know what your father told you?'

'You mean about if I break my neck it will be my own fault?'

'Yes.'

'Well, I shouldn't grumble; it's my own neck, anyway.'

Biggles looked at him doubtfully. 'All right,' he said slowly at last. 'I suppose there's no way of getting rid of you.'

'You've said it,' Ginger told him cheerfully.

Chapter 7
Warned Out

The Vandal circled gracefully and dropped lightly on to the smooth waters of the Holtenau Seaplane Station, at Kiel, the German naval base of wartime memory*, and taxied slowly past several machines that rode at moorings, towards the Custom House.

'Well, we're over the ditch, anyway,' observed Biggles to Algy, who sat beside him.

Eight days had elapsed since their decision to explore the Baltic coast had been made, eight days of exasperating delays, while their papers were being prepared. The party had now increased to four, for Biggles would not risk travelling so far afield without Smyth, their efficient mechanic, who now shared the cabin with Ginger.

'The thing I don't like about this show is that we've got to travel under our proper names,' muttered Algy, as they made fast to the slipway. 'That doesn't matter very much as far as I am concerned, I know, but Blackbeard knows your name, and so do some of the others, and the chances are that they are over here somewhere at this very minute; you say the chances of running into them or of their hearing your name mentioned, are remote, but I don't agree with you. There are only one or two seaplane stations in Germany, and you know how news travels. People, flying

---

* The First World War 1914–1918.

people at any rate, are bound to come quizzing round a British machine; we should do the same thing to a German kite* in England – in fact, we've done it more than once.'

'Suppose Blackbeard does learn that I'm here, what of it? He cannot very well have us arrested for just being here, if our papers are in order, as they are; the British Consul would want to know why. In any case I think the chances are against anyone even noticing our names; they will mean nothing to the people in the Passport Office. We couldn't fake our passports, anyway, so we had to travel under our real names or not at all.'

'You're right there, but I don't agree about not spotting our names. On the Continent people pay a good deal more attention to such things than we do, and if Blackbeard wanted us out of the way he'd find an excuse to get us out of the way, don't make any mistake about that; if you don't know German methods by this time it's about time you did.'

'We're here, so it's a bit late in the day to argue about that,' replied Biggles shortly. 'Let us report in and get filled up with petrol. If any questions are asked you know the story – we're just on a pleasure cruise round the Baltic. Let's get fixed up and have a bite of food.'

The formalities proved far less exacting than they expected; indeed, if the attitude of the officials could be taken as an indication, they were more than welcome in the country. Their Journey Log was stamped, and they were cleared by Customs with a minimum of trouble or delay. Neither was there any difficulty

* Slang for aeroplane.

81

about getting their tanks filled with oil and petrol. The officer who examined and 'cleared' the machine, in reply to their enquiry, told them in quite good English that they would get excellent food at the aerodrome café, and pointed it out to them.

Accordingly they all made their way towards it, and were soon carving some excellent Frankfurter sausage, with new bread, butter and potatoes.

There were very few people in the place; one or two mechanics in overalls, an obvious sightseer, and a couple of fellows who might have been club pilots. The English party attracted little or no attention.

They heard a machine come in and land while they were rounding off a well enjoyed meal with cheese, but they paid no attention to it. A moment later, as a voice reached them from outside, Biggles suddenly stiffened, and moved his chair quickly so that his back was towards the door.

'Go on eating,' he said quietly, 'and don't stare. Order coffee, Algy, and on no account mention my name. Speak quietly and it may not be noticed that we are English.'

Algy, after Biggles' first half dozen words, glanced towards the door. A man was looking in through the glass panels, as if in search of somebody. It was Blackbeard. He pushed the door open and entered, speaking quickly to the waiter. He spoke, of course, in German, so they could not understand what he said.

The waiter, evidently in reply to some question, shook his head, and then departed, to return a moment later with two tankards of beer which he set on the table beside Blackbeard. The door opened again and another man joined him; Algy thought it was one of the crew of the flying boat, but he was not quite sure. They settled themselves comfortably in their chairs and began a low conversation.

'This is going to be awkward,' breathed Biggles. 'If we go he is bound to see me, and we can't stay here indefinitely without an excuse.'

'We'll have some more coffee,' replied Algy quietly, and gave the order to the waiter.

'We were fools to come to this place,' ventured Biggles, after half an hour had elapsed and still Blackbeard and his companion showed no signs of moving. 'We should have known that if he was about he would be certain to come here; I expect all the pilots use this place.'

A movement in front of him caught his eye. He glanced up and saw that he was sitting opposite to a large wall mirror that bore an advertisement for beer. It was not that, however, that made him catch his breath; Blackbeard was looking straight at his reflection in the glass. As Biggles looked up he looked away and resumed the conversation with his companion in a perfectly normal voice.

Whether he had been recognized or not Biggles had no means of knowing, but very shortly afterwards Blackbeard rose, threw some money on the table, and with a parting word to the waiter, left the room with his companion.

'Have they gone?' asked Biggles as the door closed behind them.

Algy nodded. 'Think he spotted you?'

'I don't know,' replied Biggles slowly. 'He's a cunning devil. If he did see me he didn't blink an eyelid.'

'What had we better do?'

'Watch where he goes.'

'That's it,' declared Ginger, getting up, 'leave it to me!'

'But—' began Algy.

'Ginger's right,' interposed Biggles swiftly, 'he is far less likely to attract attention. Off you go, Ginger; slip back here as soon as he goes.'

Ginger was out of the door like a shot – hands in his pockets, whistling nonchalantly between his teeth.

'I don't like letting him loose like that,' Biggles went on as Ginger disappeared from view, 'but he's as sharp as a needle and can afford to take chances that we could not. He'd get away with anything. I'm beginning to like the young blighter.'

'So am I,' confessed Algy – 'hullo, who's this? It's the passport chap, and he's coming over here.'

'So! Gentlemens, you have eaten well, yes?' observed the officer as he strolled over to their table with a benevolent smile.

'Very well indeed, thanks. Have a drink?' invited Biggles.

'That is kind of you; a lager beer, I think, if you please.'

Biggles ordered the drink. 'Won't you sit down?' he said.

'Thank you, no, I must not stay. Work I must, always the work.'

Biggles watched him closely; he felt that the man had come to them with a definite object, and wondered what it was. He was soon to know.

'You go back to England now, yes?' asked the German, still smiling.

'Not just yet; we've only just come over.'

'Which way you go; to Sweden is it, yes?'

'No! We were going to see a bit of the coast; up towards Danzig you know.'

The German screwed his face into a grimace. 'But that is not good,' he said. 'We are having very bad weather reports from there now. I have one now, to-day; already they have snow.'

'We don't mind a bit of rough weather.'

'It will be better I think if you took a course to the west. If you have bad weather, and are forced down perhaps, it may be said that we gave you no weather report.'

Biggles drew a deep breath. 'So that's it, is it?' he thought. Then aloud, 'Well, we aren't really particular. We'll just have a flip round, and if we see bad weather ahead we'll come back here. Then we shall probably move either towards home or Sweden.'

'That would be much, much better,' the German replied smilingly, but there was no humour in his steely grey eyes. 'We do our best to avoid accidents,' he added as an afterthought.

'So do we,' Biggles told him.

'You stay here the night?'

'Probably. Our plans are not quite settled as a matter of fact; we just fly when we feel like it.'

'So! I must go,' said the German draining his tank-ard and rising. 'I think, Major Bigglesworth, you follow my advice, yes? You will find the weather better to the west.'

Biggles smiled. 'Righto,' he said. 'Thanks for warning us.'

'No thanks are necessary; it is our duty to take care of our guests. *Guten abend**.'

---

* German: Good evening.

'You can take care of your guests all right,' Biggles muttered softly after his retreating form, and then to Algy, 'Well, that's their first card; it's a warning, and a fair one. What he has said in actual fact is, get out while the going's good. Did you notice the way he dropped my name? He did that deliberately.'

Algy nodded. 'Yes,' he said, 'it's as clear as daylight. If we head east after this we are heading for trouble.'

An aero engine burst into life in the harbour, died down for a moment, and then burst into a full-throated roar as the machine took off.

'That's our friend Blackbeard I'll bet,' breathed Biggles.

The door opened and Ginger hurried across to them.

'He's gone,' he said.

'Then let's follow him. We'll see which direction he goes, anyway!' declared Biggles, springing to his feet.

'Are you telling me?' drawled Ginger. 'I'll say you'd be lucky.'

'What do you mean?'

'Go and take a look. They've moored a barge right across our nose.'

Biggles paid the bill and walked quickly to the door, which overlooked the harbour. An ejaculation of alarm broke from his lips as he looked through the glass panelled door. Right across the nose of the Vandal had been moored a small, black seagoing barge; another, which had evidently just come into the harbour, was drifting broadside on with the current straight towards the amphibian. A man stood in the stern with a long sweep, presumably trying to steer his craft clear of the aeroplane, but either by accident or design he was making matters worse.

Biggles' lips set in a straight line. 'Come on,' he snapped, 'they're going to crash us,' and started running as fast as his game ankle would permit towards the harbour, closely followed by the others.

It looked as if they would be too late, for the moving barge was not more than a dozen yards away, and the stationary one effectually barred any progress of the machine in a forward direction.

'Swing the prop, Smyth!' yelled Biggles, taking a running jump into the cockpit. Smyth leapt for the propeller. 'Wing tip – get to the wing tip somebody!' shouted Biggles, frantically winding the self-starter.

Ginger saw what was required instantly. He slithered along the lower plane to the wing tip, and reaching out, fended the machine away from the barge with all his strength. For a few seconds it was touch and go. The lightly floating aeroplane swung away from the vessel under Ginger's pressure, and he slid along the leading edge of the plane, still holding the machine off; then, as it swung round, he jumped on to the nose and pushed the machine clear, bringing its nose round towards the open sea. The engine came to life, and with stick and rudder hard over, Biggles drove the Vandal clear of the narrow gap just as the barge crunched down upon the slipway. The danger was past; dire calamity had been averted by a few seconds of time, for had they delayed their departure from the café by a single minute, the amphibian would inevitably have been crushed like an eggshell.

The Passport Officer came running down the slipway from his office, shouting abuse at the bargee and apologies to Biggles. 'They are careless ones,' he said, 'there was very nearly an accident.'

'Yes,' replied Biggles grimly, 'so I noticed; we'll be

more careful in future. Accident my eye,' he growled to the others. 'That was a nicely timed scheme to put us out of action, and it would have looked like an accident if we hadn't been slick. Well, that sets our clock right; we know just what to expect in future. We must never leave the machine without a guard over her. I'm afraid it's no use going after Blackbeard now,' he went on. 'He's miles away. What sort of machine was he flying, Ginger?'

'A low wing monoplane on floats; it looked like a two or three-seater. It was a type I haven't seen before so I couldn't recognize it, but it had a biplane tail unit which should make it conspicuous. It was a German machine; I noticed its nationality markings. There was a swastika under the wing tips and on the fuselage; its letters were D-XXYA.'

'Good. We shall know it again if we see it.' While he had been speaking Biggles had gone through into the cabin and reached towards the locker in which the maps were kept. He started as he opened it. 'Hullo,' he said, 'have you been to this locker, Ginger?'

'No.'

'Have you, Smyth – or you, Algy?'

'No.'

'My word, they don't waste time then; they searched the ship while we were in the café. I distinctly remember the number of the map I left on top; it's at the bottom now.'

'The Boche* is thorough if nothing else, as you should know,' Algy told him. 'You remember what I said when we landed here.'

Biggles nodded. 'Yes, and the sooner we're out of it

---

* Slang: offensive term for a German, now out of use.

the better,' he said. 'It begins to look as if Blackbeard recognized me all right. Whether he did or not it has been made quite clear that flying visitors aren't popular here.'

'Which way are you going?' asked Algy.

'East, but I am going west first. When we take off we'll head due west so that they will think we have decided to get back to England, but as soon as we are out of sight we'll swing round and work our way back towards the east; we'll strike the coast again higher up.'

'What about petrol?'

'We'll try and make Danzig; we shall be able to get it there without difficulty. Danzig is a free port.'

They took off without further delay, and following the course they had planned, struck the north German coast again near Rugen Island. They saw nothing of interest so they passed on, flying straight along the coast, searching the ground every inch of the way for likely landing grounds for marine aircraft, or hangars that might house such giant machines as the one they had seen on the east coast of England. But they saw nothing of a suspicious nature; occasionally they passed a small fishing vessel, and once they saw a battleship far out to sea; that was all.

Daylight was failing by the time they reached Hela, at the mouth of the Gulf of Danzig, and Biggles was just reaching for the throttle in order to glide lower when the engine coughed, spluttered, and then cut right out. He was not in the least alarmed, thinking that the main tank had merely run dry, so he switched over to the rear main tank. Nothing happened, and it took him a couple of seconds to realize that something was wrong. He immediately switched over to the gravity tank* and was relieved to hear the engine pick up again. 'Tell Smyth to look at that rear tank!' he shouted to Algy, with an unpleasant suspicion forming in his mind.

Algy obediently crawled through the hatch into the cabin, but was back in a couple of minutes.

'It's empty!' he shouted.

Biggles frowned. 'I saw them fill it!' he yelled.

'So did I, but they must have emptied it again while we were in the café.'

Then, without warning, the engine cut right out again; the propeller gave a final kick and stopped, and it was obvious from the way it did it that the gravity tank had also run dry.

Biggles understood the position at once. 'They nearly emptied the gravity tank, too,' he said in the silence that followed the engine's failure. 'They left us just enough petrol to get off so that we should not suspect anything and examine the other tanks.'

There was only one course open to him; he tilted the nose of the machine down towards the water, which fortunately was quite smooth, at the same time swinging round towards the beach which lay a few hundred yards away to the right. 'Have we any spare petrol on board?' he asked as the Vandal ran to a standstill on the water. 'I don't remember seeing any.'

'No, I didn't think we should need it, and we already had plenty of weight up with four people on board.'

'As you remarked at Kiel, it's time I understood the

_____
* A small tank of fuel, which is literally gravity-fed into the engine without the aid of a pump, for use in an emergency.

Hun*; I should have suspected that something like this would happen. Think what a nice mess we should have been in if we had taken that fellow's advice and headed back for England; we should now be derelict just about in the middle of the North Sea. If a breeze happened to blow up during the night, that would have been the end of the Vandal – and us.

'As luck would have it we are here, thank goodness, but it is going to be awkward. If there was a vessel about going in the direction of Danzig I'd ask for a tow, but there isn't, so we shall have to try and attract the attention of the people ashore. I see several houses about, fishermen's cottages, by the look of them, and I can see several boats pulled up on the beach. We daren't risk mooring out here on the open sea in case a storm happens to blow up. One of us will have to try and get ashore and get some petrol from somewhere or else hire a fisherman to tow us down to Danzig; it can't be more than five or six miles away.'

It was clear that there would be no difficulty in attracting the attention of people on the shore, for a number had already collected on the beach, evidently having seen the flying boat land, and in reply to its distress signals, two or three boats at once put out. To arrange for a tow to Danzig, however, proved impossible. Conversation, such as it was, was slow, and most of it was carried on by signs. At the end of ten minutes, the position, as far as the airmen could make it out, was this. Not one of the fishing boats had an engine. There was no wind so it would not be possible to travel under sail. To row to Danzig at that particular

* Slang: derogatory term for a German, now out of use.

hour was impossible on account of a strong current that was set against them. Further, the Vandal had no riding lights and the fishermen said there was a chance of their being run down in the darkness by traffic going to and from the port.

'It looks as if there is only one thing for it,' observed Biggles, 'and that is to get them to tow us ashore here. There doesn't seem to be much surf and there should be plenty of hands to pull us high and dry. We can spend the night ashore, in the cabin if necessary, and as soon as it is light three of us will go and fetch some petrol from Danzig while the other remains on guard. If we can hire a motor vehicle of any sort to fetch a load of petrol, it should be simple enough. We are bound to be able to get food here, anyway.'

So it was arranged. The boatmen, as soon as they had grasped what was wanted, got a line over the nose of the Vandal and towed her to the shore, where the wheels were lowered, and many willing hands pulled her high and dry near the ramshackle boathouses beyond the reach of heavy seas. Biggles distributed some money amongst the helpers, who seemed more than satisfied, and it was quite dark by the time everything was settled. There was no sleeping accommodation available, but food and coffee in abundance at the chandler's store, to which they repaired and spent part of the evening. What was really more important, there was a telephone on which Biggles was able to speak to the British Consulate Office in Danzig and explain their predicament, with a result that it was arranged for a consignment of aviation spirit and oil to be sent out to them, by lorry, immediately.

'I shall soon want some more money if this sort of thing goes on,' remarked Biggles as they made their way back to the machine; 'I paid for one load at Kiel this morning, so this trip is going to work out expensive if we're not careful. Taking it all in all though, I think we've got away with it today very well, and as far as our present position is concerned, I don't know but that we aren't as well off as if we had gone on to Danzig. There is certainly less chance of awkward questions being asked.' The petrol arrived shortly afterwards, and after attending to the refuelling of the machine, they settled themselves down to pass the night as comfortably as they could.

Chapter 8
A Chapter of Adventures

Biggles awoke from a deep sleep and sat up abruptly, wide awake on the instant, wondering if he had really heard what he thought he had heard, or if he had been dreaming. No, the sound came again from afar off, the low, rhythmic palpitating beat of a multi-engined aeroplane. He slung the tarpaulin with which he had covered himself to one side, and ran out of the boathouse in which he had decided to sleep in preference to the cramped cabin. He tapped sharply on the Vandal's hull.

'Stand by, everybody,' he snapped crisply. 'Algy, come outside, quickly; what do you make of this, hark!'

It was still dark, but the stars were paling, and a wan light spread over the eastern sky in promise of the day to come. The distant roar of the aeroplane reached their ears clearly, although it came from a long way away, as if the machine was flying at a great height, but it was obviously travelling in their direction from the west.

'What do you make of it Smyth?' asked Biggles.

'Sounds like five or six Mercedes* engines to me, sir, but there is something funny about them; they seem sort of – muffled.'

'I thought so,' replied Biggles tersely. 'It's that big

---

* *Mercedes Benz*, German manufacturer of aircraft engines during World War One.

machine all right – there she is.' He grabbed Algy by the shoulder and pointed with outstretched finger at a tiny, gleaming point of light that had been caught in the sun's rays. The sun was still below the horizon to the watchers on the ground, but the machine, by reason of its great altitude, came within the region of its upflung rays.

As they spoke, the noise of the engines died away suddenly, but the tiny point of light held on its course like a shooting star. 'That's it,' muttered Biggles, 'they've switched the silencers full on now while they pass Danzig. Come on, after it. Start up Smyth. Algy, and you Ginger, take station where you can see that machine and don't take your eyes off it until I'm in the air, or we may not be able to pick it up again.'

The Vandal's engine started at the second swing, and Smyth clung to a wing tip to drag her round facing the water. Biggles raised the wheels as the machine became water-borne, and then churned up a foaming wake as he sped across the smooth surface of the water.

'How high is she do you think?' he yelled, nodding towards the higher machine.

'Ten thousand for a guess.'

'That's about what I put it. We can't climb up to her without losing speed – not that we particularly want to; she'll have to come down sooner or later. All we have to do is to keep her in sight, but we must keep out of sight of her ourselves if we can.'

Then began a chase which seemed interminable. Hour after hour passed, the big machine maintaining its altitude, with the Vandal skimming along a few hundred feet above the ground. Biggles was flying on full throttle in order to keep up with the other, although he realized that the big machine was probably only cruising. Their course lay due east, and for a long time it lay over open water, although the coast was always visible in the distance. A large town, which Biggles knew could only be Köningsberg, in East Prussia*, loomed up on the horizon, and slipped away behind, after which their course became overland.

Another two hours passed, and Biggles began to get worried, for he knew that they were reaching the limit of the Vandal's endurance range. He still had plenty of petrol to continue the chase, but if he went on any further he would be unable to return to Danzig** without landing and refuelling, a procedure that he knew might give rise to an awkward situation. Looking at his map, and working out the distance in conjunction with the speed of the Vandal, a quick mental calculation told him that they must have passed over Prussia, cut across a corner of Lithuania and Poland, and were now actually on the Russian frontier, if not actually in Russia. The country below seemed deserted, the one or two small villages they passed occurring only at long intervals; not by a single landmark could they judge their position to within a hundred miles. Presently a small lake appeared below, but it was unmarked on their map and told them nothing. Then a larger lake appeared, so large that they could not see the opposite bank.

'Look out!' cried Algy suddenly. 'She's coming down.'

Biggles looked about hurriedly for some place of concealment. There is only one form of cover in the

* This area now within the Russian Federation.
** Now Poland.

96

air, and that is provided by clouds, but at that moment there was not a single cloud in the sky. Just in front of them lay a great forest, spreading round on either side of the lake. At its western extremity the ground was open, and appeared to be uninhabited, for they could see no signs of human habitation. Biggles put his nose down towards it, although there was no time to make a close examination of the surface of the ground if they were to avoid being seen by the crew of the now rapidly dropping giant. He cut the throttle and lowered his wheels, and picking the most open space he could see near the wall of the forest, made a rather bumpy landing.

'Thank God there were no rabbit holes,' he murmured fervently as he kicked over the rudder and taxied close up to the trees. 'Quick everybody, get some branches, grass, anything you can lay hands on and throw it over the top wing.'

It was the work of only two or three minutes to cover the white wings and tail planes of the Vandal with greenery, and then, keeping in the shelter of the trees, they watched the big bomber glide down towards the lake. They did not actually see it land, for the forest, which lay between them and the water, obstructed their view, but they knew that it could not be more than a mile or two away, for it had passed over them at a very low altitude.

'What now?' asked Algy, looking inquiringly at Biggles.

'We had better do a bit of thinking,' was the reply. 'In the first place I estimate that we have just about enough petrol to get back as far as Königsberg, although what sort of reception we shall get there I hardly like to think; still, it can't be helped. Next, we may have been heard by somebody when we landed, or we may be heard if we try to take off again. We're skating on thin ice, make no mistake about that. Our papers may be in order, and all that sort of thing, but it won't count for much if we are caught spying – and we shall have a job to find a reasonable excuse for being here. Still, we haven't come all this way for nothing; what we've got to find out is just what sort of place there is here, how many of those machines there are, and how much accommodation. That is what we want to know. If we can find out what they ultimately hope to achieve, how often they fly to England, and where their landing grounds are there, so much the better. It seems to me that there are two courses open to us. The first is to take off again, fly round the lake, learning as much as we can, and then make full out for home, but the most we can hope to discover if we do that, is how many machines they have, and only then if they happen to be moored out on the water; we might be able to count the hangars – there must be more than one of those machines here. The second idea would be to hide the machine rather more effectively, and do a bit of scouting on foot. That, to my mind, is the best plan, but of course it is far more dangerous. If we were caught, we should be caught red-handed, and it would be Siberia* for the lot of us – perhaps worse.'

'You're telling me,' interposed Ginger quietly.

'I'm telling everybody,' replied Biggles shortly, 'but as you are all in this as well as me you have some say in the matter. Well, which is it to be?'

'Scouting on foot,' replied Ginger quickly.

---

* The bleak snow-covered Russian region of Siberia was where many prisoners were kept.

'I agree,' said Algy.

'What suits you suits me, sir,' declared Smyth.

'All right; scouting on foot it is. In that case I propose to split up the party. You will be on one side, Algy, and I shall be on the other. Then, if the scouting party is caught, that still leaves a pilot with the machine to fly back to the Air Ministry and report what has happened. I suggest therefore that you, Algy, and Smyth, stay here with the machine, while Ginger and I take a walk. Stand by for a quick take-off in case we come back in a hurry.'

'As you like,' agreed Algy.

The machine was pulled into a narrow glade amongst the drooping fir trees of the forest, with her nose pointing towards the open ground. They then sat down and ate the emergency rations they had brought with them from England.

'We shall have to leave here tomorrow at the latest,' observed Biggles thoughtfully, as he munched a biscuit. 'We can't live on air, and it would be too risky to try and get food about here. We should be spotted for foreigners instantly.'

The meal, such as it was, was soon finished, and Biggles rose, throwing his cap and goggles into the cockpit. 'One last thing,' he told Algy seriously, 'if we are not back here by this time tomorrow, you'll know something serious has happened; in that case make for home as fast as you can and tell Taglen, at the Air Ministry, what has happened.'

Algy nodded.

'Right then. Cheerio. Come on, Ginger,' said Biggles, and set off through the forest in the direction of the lake. For a long time they walked in silence, seeing nothing of interest, and then suddenly they perceived the steely blue gleam of water through the tree trunks.

'Steady now,' he whispered, but the warning was unnecessary; Ginger was gliding from tree to tree, with the stealth of an Indian, a few yards ahead of him. He saw him stop, staring, and then beckon him on with a curious gesture.

He was not altogether surprised at the sight that met his eyes, for he was half prepared for something of the sort, yet he caught his breath sharply. At the far side of the lake, or rather, on the opposite side of a wide arm of it which at this point drove deep into the forest, was a long row of enormous, squat hangars, built at the water's edge. In front of them, riding at anchor, were ten or a dozen of the great flying boats, with several smaller marine aircraft dotted about them. They could not actually count the number of machines for they were more or less in line across the lake, and they were looking straight down the line; but it was not the machines that shook Biggles so much as the activity going on ashore. Log-built houses and workshops were everywhere, with scores of men moving about them, and the dull clamour of a thousand tools reached their ears. As they watched, the air began to vibrate with the roar of engines under test, while the door of a hangar was dragged open, and another monster slid down a slipway to the water.

'I'm going to have a closer look at this,' muttered Biggles, and his methodical mind made him add, 'If by any chance we get parted, come back to this spot. You can mark the place by that pine tree over there, the one with the broken bough.'

'OK, chief,' breathed Ginger, still staring at the scene across the bay.

'We'd better strike inland a bit or we may be seen,' went on Biggles, and began working his way slowly towards the flying boats, keeping parallel with the shore, but a little distance from it. He noticed that an open space had been cut through the trees just ahead, and presently saw the reason; a track had been cut for a light railway, which seemed to run down to the seaplane station in one direction and into the mainland in the other. There was a siding at the point where they actually came upon it, with a row of trucks on the rails, but all was quiet, and a little careful scouting showed that the track was deserted.

'Come on, let's cross over,' he said quietly.

The trucks lay immediately in their path, and rather than go round them, which would have meant exposing themselves on the open track rather longer than they cared to, they started squeezing between them. They were actually in the act of doing this when the dull thud of horses' hooves sounded close at hand from the forest on the opposite side of the track, and a man's voice called loudly. Biggles acted on the instinct of self-preservation. There was no time to go forward or back, for the man seemed to be right upon them, so he pulled himself over the side of the nearest truck and fell in a heap inside. What happened to Ginger he did not know, but from the sounds he heard he gathered that he had done the same thing in the next truck, an assumption which afterwards proved to be correct. Not until he was inside the truck did he realize that it was half full of rough sawn timber, pine logs, the transport of which was apparently the purpose of the line, but he wedged himself between them, going as far as pulling a couple of the logs over his body.

He heard the horse pulled up as its rider reached the track. A hail rang through the forest, and he started as another voice answered from somewhere desperately close; it seemed to come from the front end of the stationary train, and he broke into a perspiration when he realized that someone must have been there all the time. The two men began talking, and although he could not understand the conversation, it seemed to Biggles that the rider was reprimanding the other for failure to do something. They were still talking when an engine whistled in the distance, and he stiffened as a new possibility struck him. He hoped that the approaching train would pass them on the other set of rails, but whether it did or did not, it was utterly impossible for him to abandon his hiding place now without being seen. His heart sank as he heard the train slowing down, but he was quite unprepared for what followed. There was a frightful crash, and his head struck the back of the truck with a force that nearly dislocated his neck. The engine had evidently arrived to pick up the trucks, and at the terrifying prospect of being carried to an unknown and possibly distant destination, he nearly risked everything by jumping clear and making a dash for the forest. Had he been alone he would certainly have done so, but he could not leave Ginger, nor could he make his plan known to him without attracting the attention of the two men, who were still talking not a dozen yards away.

He was still feverishly turning the matter over in his mind when the truck in which he lay began to move, slowly, but with ever increasing speed, yet all he could do was to lie still and hope for the best. They had travelled about half a mile, as near as he could judge, when it began to slow down again; he could stand the strain no longer.

'Ginger,' he said crisply, 'are you there, Ginger?'

A sudden anxiety assailed him as no answering call came from the next truck. 'Ginger,' he said again, more loudly.

Still there was no reply.

Swiftly he thrust aside the logs and risked a peep over the edge of the truck; but he was back on the floor again instantly, knowing only too well what had happened. There were no more trucks behind him; he was in the end one. The train must have been uncoupled at the very truck into which he had climbed; the engine had picked up one half of the train and left the rest behind. It had taken him with it and left Ginger back on the siding in the forest. What was even more unnerving was the fact that the train had pulled in to what seemed to be the very middle of the seaplane station. He had only had time for a brief glimpse, yet all around him as far as he could see were wooden buildings, like a vast lumber camp.

He lay quite still and tried to work the thing out in his mind; he had been anxious to gain a closer view of the secret aerodrome, but this was certainly a good deal closer than he liked. Somehow or other he would have to get clear again as soon as possible and return to the tree with the broken branch, and he thanked his lucky star that he had had the foresight to make an arrangement against such an emergency. Ginger, he knew, would work his way back to it at the first opportunity.

For a long time he lay quite still while he could hear people moving about, sometimes passing within a yard of him as they walked along the track. Then came a voice that made his skin tingle; there was no mistaking it. It was the voice of Blackbeard, and to his amazement he spoke in English.

'Hullo, Darton, what are you doing back here?' he said.

'You might well ask,' was the reply, accompanied by the slamming of a door.

Biggles quivered again, for it was the voice of his late gaoler in the Northumbrian house.

'Yes, it was that swine of an Englishman, Bigglesmore, or whatever his name is,' went on the man, whose name was evidently Darton. 'He caused a nice old mess – I suppose you've heard about it?'

'I heard that you let him get away and the Boss had to do some quick thinking – had to abandon two of our bases over the other side.'

'Let him get away! I like that. Some kid set the whole works on fire. The Boss has sent me back here for punishment. I wasn't to know that the fellow had his pals with him.'

'Pals did you say?'

'Yes, a couple of them at least; one of 'em's only a kid. The little swine nearly broke my legs with a cudgel. If I ever lay hands on him I'll wring his blamed neck like a rabbit's.' From the tone of his voice there was little doubt but that he meant what he said.

'Well, it was a bad business,' went on Blackbeard, 'a lot of good work undone. How did you get here?'

'Flew back in number fourteen the night before last. I wanted to stay in England to find this fellow Bigglesmore, but the Boss wouldn't let me; I'd have settled for his hash once and for all.'

'You'd have been wasting your time looking for him in England.'

'How's that?'

'He's over here.'

'Who told you that?'

'Nobody. I saw him myself, yesterday, at Holtenau.'

'Were you drunk?'

'No,' replied Blackbeard curtly, 'and kindly refrain from being unpleasant or I shall tell you nothing more.'

'Sorry, go on, what did you do? Sock him—?'

'No, but I—'

The crash of buffers, as the train began to move again, cut off the rest of the conversation, much to Biggles' disgust, but by the merest fluke he had gathered some very useful information. It was as well to know that there were at least two men in the camp who could recognize him – Blackbeard, and Darton, his late captor.

The train pulled up again with a jerk that shook every tooth in Biggles' head. There was a hiss of escaping steam, voices calling to each other, and then silence. The late afternoon wore on and it began to grow dark. He was just beginning to hope that the train had been abandoned for the rest of the day and was thinking of risking a peep, when the sound of returning voices reached his ears. Someone began to give orders, the words being punctuated every now and then by the crash of timber. Then, without the slightest warning, the truck in which he was lying was tilted over, and he was flung headlong out. Before he could make the slightest effort to save himself, he was sliding, slipping and rolling down an apparently bottomless pit. Instinctively he flung up his arms to protect his face, but a smashing blow struck him on the head, and he knew no more.

Chapter 9
Ginger Strikes

When he recovered consciousness it was quite dark, and it took him some minutes to remember what had happened and where he was. The fall had been so sudden that there had been no time to see anything, and the crack he received on the head from one of the logs – for he had no doubt as to what had put him out of action – had settled any immediate anxiety on the point. He sat up, feeling rather giddy, and felt his head tenderly, but he was relieved to find that the injury was not so severe as he had expected, although a nasty lump under a sticky cake of hair told him that the skin of his scalp had been broken.

He looked around in the dim starlight, and saw that he had been tipped out with the logs into a deep gully, which was straddled by a trestle bridge. Luckily he had almost rolled under the bridge, which may have accounted for his not having been seen by the men operating the trucks. For what purpose the logs were required, or what lay at the bottom of the gully, he could not see, nor did he waste time trying to find out. He had learned quite a lot, not so much as he had hoped, but sufficient to report to the authorities in England, who would no doubt put their specially-trained sleuths on the track. His immediate desire now was to get back to the Vandal with the least possible delay, and put the North Sea between him and Blackbeard.

His watch had been smashed by the fall and he had no idea of the time, but he felt that it must be somewhere about midnight; he did not think it could be after that hour. Where was Ginger? The thought worried him a good deal, although he tried to thrust the matter aside until he was in a position to deal with it. He would get back as quickly as possible to the tree with the broken branch; if Ginger was not there then he would go on to the Vandal; that he would find him at one of the two places he felt sure.

The business of getting back up to the railway line was no easy matter. Hundreds of logs lay loosely about, just as they had fallen, and at every step one or more would become detached and go crashing down to the bottom of the gully. Once he started a whole avalanche, and was nearly carried down with it, but he saved himself just in time; somewhere, not far away, a hound started baying – an unpleasant sound. The noise he made climbing up to the bridge seemed to occasion no alarm, however, and he came to the conclusion that the logs often fell of their own accord, and the crash of tumbling timbers was a common sound. At last he reached the top of the pile and with some difficulty dragged himself up a lattice-work trestle to the bridge. A quick glance up and down showed that it was deserted, but a number of lights in the distance revealed the position of the camp. He also noticed something else, something that filled him with dismay. In the opposite direction the line ran out on to a small promontory, so it was no good going that way. What was even worse, the first buildings of the camp seemed to begin at the far end of the bridge on which he stood, so that he would have to pass through them in order to escape. There was no alternative, so he started off, making as little noise as possible, eyes probing the darkness ahead, keeping a keen lookout for sentries.

He came to a place where the line swung round to the right and the whole waterfront lay open to his view in the starlight. Twelve of the giant bombers were now moored to iron buoys, in two lines. Several smaller machines were moored about them, some close to the hangars and some out on the open water. He saw the machine in which Blackbeard had flown to Holtenau moored close to a wharf at the far end of the line of hangars. Ginger had described it exactly. Automatically, with the precision of long experience in reconnaissance, Biggles made a mental note of everything he could see, hangars, workshops, test benches, and the like, and then, satisfied with his inspection and the information he had gained, he proceeded towards the camp. As he approached it he saw at once that he was faced with a very difficult proposition, for the camp radiated fanwise, from the very end of the railway, and it was impossible to reach the forest beyond without going through it. If people were still moving about, it would be impossible to avoid being seen. There was no cover of which he could take advantage, anywhere along the track. Still, he could not remain where he was, for sooner or later somebody would certainly come along and see him, and there was no point in going back. If he went forward he could adopt one or two methods of procedure. He could either walk straight down the middle of the track trusting that if he was seen he would be taken for an employee, or he could creep from house to house, and avoid meeting anyone face to face. If he adopted the latter course, and *was* seen, then his very actions themselves would be sufficient to arouse suspicion. Still walking on, he decided to compromise between the two; he would walk straight down the track, but would turn aside if he saw anyone coming. If he was challenged he would simply have to make a bolt for the forest.

He reached the first buildings without seeing a soul, but a moment later two men stepped out of a doorway not five yards away; there was no time to turn aside, so he walked straight on, passing so close to the men that he could have touched them. As far as he could gather they took not the slightest notice of him, although he did not turn round after he had passed them. Then a party of six or seven crossed an area of light in front of an open window about fifty yards ahead; they appeared to be coming in his direction, so he turned sharply to the right into a convenient passage between the houses, and then again to the left in order to maintain his general direction towards the forest.

He had almost reached it – he was, in fact, actually passing the last block of buildings – when three men, in earnest conversation, appeared round a corner in front of him. One voice could be heard above the others; it was Blackbeard's. To pass without being seen was an utter impossibility, and there was no side turning in which he could conceal himself. The realization of these two facts flashed through his head in a split second. Some of the houses had rough porches built around the doors, and without the slightest hesitation he stepped into the first one he reached. It was quite a shallow affair, not more than a couple of feet deep, and provided scanty shelter, but he pressed himself against the dark door in order to make the best of it. Before he could take any steps to prevent it, the door, which had evidently not been closed, swung inwards, and he pitched headfirst inside. He was on his feet in an instant, hands raised to repel the attack which he felt sure must follow, but nothing happened. The room was in darkness except for the faint reflected light that came from outside, and he just had time to swing the door in place before Blackbeard and his companions reached it. Stone cold with the nervous tension of the moment, he stood stock still and waited for them to pass; but they did not pass. On reaching the door they stopped, and it was instantly apparent that one of them at least was about to enter. He knew this and acted with the speed of the experienced air fighter.

The three men were now actually standing in the doorway, talking in tones which suggested a mild argument; at any instant they might enter, so he took a couple of paces into the room and peered around. It was furnished as an office. A large desk, with a shaded electric light over it, occupied the centre; filing cabinets took up most of the walls, except that part which was taken up by the window overlooking the street. Against the far wall, however, there was one of those tall cupboards used for storing stationery. He reached it in a couple of paces and swung the door open. A few large envelopes lay on the floor; higher up there was a shelf with a number of small boxes on it; between the shelf and the floor there was just sufficient room for a man to stand upright and close the door behind him, provided he was slim. All this he saw at a glance, and it was the work of a moment to step inside and pull the door to; there was no time to latch it, for even as he pulled the door towards him the outside door was thrown open. An electric switch clicked and the room was flooded with light. Still arguing, in a language Biggles did not understand, the three men walked into the room. Blackbeard, whose office it seemed to be judging by his actions, threw his cap into a corner, and flinging himself into the largest chair, rested his feet on the desk. He took a cigar from his pocket, bit off the end and spat it across the room. Of the other two men, one was Darton; the third was a stranger, but evidently a pilot for he carried a flying cap in his hand. Biggles could just see this through the narrow chink of the unlatched door.

'You've got the advantage of me;' grumbled Darton presently, speaking in English for the first time; 'I can't keep pace with this damn lingo of yours. I told the Boss it was no use sending me over here; what does he think I am going to do I should like to know if I don't understand half what people say to me?'

'You'll know all in good time if I know anything about the Boss,' Blackbeard told him coolly. 'You're lucky to get off as lightly as you have, after making the mess you made of things, over there.'

'I didn't make any mess I tell you!' cried Darton indignantly. 'How was I to know Biggleston – or whatever his name is – had a gang working with him.' He cursed luridly. 'If I could get my hands on that smug faced—'

He broke off short and remained with his mouth open, an expression of inane surprise in his eyes. The reason was not hard to find. Across the room not three yards away, the man he was speaking about stood facing him.

Just how it happened Biggles never knew. Whether

111

he accidentally touched the door with his coat or sleeve, or whether a draught caught it, he could not say; nor did he bother to inquire into such insignificant details. The only thing that mattered was that the door of the cupboard, either with his assistance or on its own volition, had swung open, slowly, but just too fast for him to prevent it. Darton, who was standing opposite, saw the movement and glanced up; the expression on his face brought the others round.

Biggles was the first to move. Further effort at concealment would have been merely childish, and unfortunately the three men were between him and the door. He stepped out of the cupboard into the room.

'Well,' he said, 'here we are again.'

Blackbeard was the only one who did not move, but a slow smile spread over his face. Darton jumped to the door and swung round, revolver in hand. The third man, after a swift glance at the others, blocked the gangway between the desk and the wall. For perhaps thirty seconds the picture remained unchanged.

'I wonder if you could oblige me with a cigarette?' Biggles asked Blackbeard quietly. 'I lost my case you know.'

'With the greatest of pleasure,' replied Blackbeard, offering him his cigarette case. 'I must say you have a most disconcerting habit of turning up at unexpected places. I hope you are not going to tell me that you came *here* by accident?'

'Yes, curious to relate, that would be no more than the sober truth – at least, as far as my method of entry into this place is concerned. I won't strain your credulity by going into details though.'

'No, it would hardly be worth the effort,' Blackbeard assured him easily. 'The chief thing is, you are here, and that is really all we are concerned with. This time I imagine our mutual friend Darton will take more effective measures to ensure that you do not leave us so abruptly as you did on the last occasion. As you may well imagine, he is feeling more than a little annoyed about the way you went off, in England, without so much as saying good-bye.'

'Quite,' replied Biggles evenly, 'but there were several urgent things I had to do. You can't really complain though, because I've come back again, as you see.' He had been talking solely to gain time to think, and hardly knew what he was saying. His brain was working at feverish speed, trying to find a loophole of escape, but there was none. To employ force, unarmed as he was, against three armed men, could only end one way in real life, although it sometimes works out differently in the films.

'Yes, I'll take care of you this time,' sneered Darton. 'You talk too much, that's your trouble.'

'So do you. Stick your hands up and keep them there. I'll drop the first man who moves!'

The words, in a shrill treble, but hard as steel, cut through the room like a trumpet call; they came from the direction of the window, which was now open. Biggles had not seen it open; neither had the others; they had all been intent on the dramatic scene being enacted in the room. Even Biggles was shaken to the core and he could only stand and stare. At the open window, his head just above the sill, was Ginger. His right arm was thrust forward into the room, the hand gripping a squat automatic.

Blackbeard's burst of laughter broke the tension; it was clear that none of them took the matter seriously.

113

'Why that's the little swine who burst my shins,' roared Darton, and swung up his revolver.

There was a deafening roar and a streak of orange flame leapt across the room; it began at the window and ended at Darton's chest. The air was filled with the acrid smell of burning cordite. In the silence that followed, Darton turned slowly towards the others, a curious expression of inane surprise on his face. His lips twitched once, twice, and then he crashed face downwards on to the wooden floor.

'I warned you,' came Ginger's voice in a high falsetto, 'the next man who moves gets his. Come on, Biggles, what are you standing there for?'

Biggles crossed the room in a bound, snatching up the fallen man's revolver on the way, and dived through the window to the street.

'Keep your distance,' he told Blackbeard, 'I should be sorry to have to shoot you.' Then, with Ginger at his side, they sprinted for the forest.

They were only just in time, for the shot had been heard, and people were running up the main street towards the house. Luckily, the forest lay in the opposite direction.

'Keep to the track until we reach the siding,' Biggles panted as they ran on. 'It will be as black as pitch under the trees.'

Shouts came from the direction of the town; a whistle blew, and there were more shouts. 'Here we are,' he went on a few minutes later as they reached, the place where they had boarded the train. 'We shall have to take to the forest here. It will be hard to keep straight, but we shall have to do our best.'

'Biggles,' gasped Ginger.

'Yes, what's the matter?'

'Did I – have I killed him?'

'I don't know.'

'I felt awful – I didn't know it was loaded.'

'What! Do you mean to say you had the cheek to try and hold up the party with an empty gun?'

'That's what I thought. It was that chap's gun, too; you remember I picked it up that day we set fire to the house. I fired six shots that night, and I thought that was all it held – that's why they call 'em six-shooters.'

'Those are revolvers. Automatics hold up to a dozen, but seven is quite common.'

'There must have been seven in mine. When he pointed his revolver at me I was so scared that I pulled the trigger of mine. I thought it was his gun that had gone off till I saw him fall.'

'Well, he asked for what he got so I shouldn't worry about it,' replied Biggles shortly. 'He would have shot you, anyway. It seems to me that a fellow who pulls a gun on another chap can't complain if he gets shot himself.'

'But I hope—'

'Save your breath,' Biggles told him, 'you got me out of a nasty jam, that's the most important thing. What have you got in your hand?'

'A case I found in one of the huts. I thought there might be some information in it worth having.'

'Jumping mackerel!' Biggles looked at him in amazement. 'You certainly do think of things,' he muttered. 'Where did you get it?'

'Well, you see I was pretty worried when I discovered that the train had taken you away. The chap on the horse went off soon afterwards and I got back into the wood. I went back to the tree with the broken branch, but you weren't there, so I thought I'd better see if I could find you. As soon as it was dark I went down to those wooden huts and places and hung about there for a long time, but I couldn't see a sign of you. Then I started exploring a bit closer. The first hut I came to was a big place with maps all over the wall – I had a squint through the window. There were a lot of men in it, including the chap I shot and the other two. Then they all got up as if they were going and I saw one of them, the fellow who had done most of the talking, put some papers in a bag and put it on a shelf. Then they all went out. I slipped in and got the bag after they had gone, and then went down the back of the buildings, looking in the windows of those where there were any lights; that's how I saw you in the room with those three chaps. I could see how you were fixed too, so I thought I had better do something about it.'

'You certainly did that,' replied Biggles grimly. 'I'll buy you an aeroplane one of these days for pulling me out of that scrape. Steady now, mind your head on that branch. There's the lake on the right, that gives us our bearings. Hark!'

They stopped to listen. From different parts of the forest behind them came shouts and sharply given orders, but they were some distance away.

'It sounds as if they're going to try and find us, but we got a good start,' went on Biggles. 'We shall have to get out of this place before morning though. They'll comb every inch of it tomorrow now that they know we're here. If they do they'll find the Vandal, so we shall have to get off at the first crack of dawn. The bigger the distance we put between this place now and ourselves the better.'

'If they catch me, knowing that I've bumped off that guy—'

'They're not going to catch us,' Biggles assured him with a conviction he was far from feeling. 'We can't be very far away from the Vandal now. Ah! Here comes the moon; that's better. Yes, we're right, I remember those two holly bushes.'

Fortunately it was fairly open under the trees, and they made good progress, so it was not long before the open country loomed up beyond the edge of the forest.

'Here we are,' announced Biggles. 'Half a minute though – that's funny.' A cold hand seemed to catch his heart as he looked around the glade. Beyond all doubt it was the place where they had left the Vandal, for they could see the wheels' tracks in the loose pine needles, but the amphibian was no longer there. 'She's gone!' he cried hoarsely.

'You've sure said it,' agreed Ginger calmly.

Biggles sat down on the stump of a fallen tree. 'This is something I didn't bargain for,' he said quietly.

Chapter 10
Smyth Explains

'MAJOR BIGGLESWORTH!'

Biggles jumped as if he had been shot; the words seemed to come from the air, and the voice that uttered them seemed strangely familiar.

'Hullo yes, who's that?' he answered sharply, grabbing Ginger by the arm and hurrying to the side of the clearing ready for instant flight.

'It's all right, sir, it's me, Smyth.' There was a movement in the branches overhead, and they stared upwards. 'Just a minute, sir, I'm coming down,' went on Smyth, and presently he appeared, brushing dead twigs and pine needles from his face and hair.

'What in the name of heaven has happened?' asked Biggles quickly. 'Where's the machine – and where is Mr. Lacey?'

'He's gone, sir – they've both gone.'

'Gone! Where?'

'I'll tell you all about it, but we'd better not stay here; it isn't safe. Some soldiers have already been here.'

'Soldiers!'

'Well, they looked like it; they were either soldiers or glorified policemen. Can we find a place to hide while I tell you about it.'

'Let's go back to those holly bushes,' suggested Biggles. 'I'm not very happy about it as a hiding place, but I know of nowhere better.'

They hurried back to the place he had named, and in the inky black recesses of the hollies Smyth told his story.

'You'd been gone about an hour, I should think it would be,' he began, 'and we were keeping a strict watch when we saw some machines on the horizon. They flew up and down for a bit and then they disappeared. About ten minutes later another lot came along from a different direction – three of them. We didn't pay much attention at first, except to take a general look as we should at any aeroplane. They were flying very low, under a thousand feet I should think, and about a quarter of a mile apart. Every now and then they turned and went back in the direction from which they had come, but a bit to one side of their original course; then they'd turn again and come back. We watched them for a bit, wondering what the dickens they were doing, and then Mr Lacey said, "Those fellows are looking for something, I wonder what it can be."

'It's funny, but it didn't strike either of us that time what they *were* looking for. They were working back towards us, on another beat, in a manner of speaking, when Mr Lacey jumped up and said, "What fools we are; they're looking for us." There was nothing we could do except sit still and hope they wouldn't see us, but it was no go. We'd covered the machine up pretty well, as you know, and I don't think anyone would have noticed it from the air in the ordinary way; but these fellows were deliberately looking, and covering every inch of the ground. They were two-seaters and I could see the fellows in the back seats leaning over the side. I saw one of them spot us as clear as daylight. By a bit of bad luck he had come

119

smack over us. He was looking straight down on us and I saw him turn and tap his pilot on the shoulder, and then point. They came roaring down to about fifty feet, and I don't mind telling you we lay flat, thinking perhaps they were going to start bombing us; thank goodness they didn't. The chap who had seen us must have been in touch by wireless with the others for presently they all came circling over us, and then they turned and made off.

'Mr Lacey got into a rare state after they had gone. He said, "Those machines were making a systematic search for us, and they are not the only ones, I'll be bound. They've got wireless and they'll send an armed guard straight to this spot; we shall have to get out of it." "What about Major Bigglesworth and Ginger?" I said. Well, he sat down on that tree where you sat a minute ago and stared at the ground. "I'm dashed if I know what to do for the best," he said. "If we stay here they're bound to find us and collar the Vandal, and then we're sunk; there's no getting away from that. Yet if we take the machine away, how on earth can we let the others know what has happened; what will they do when they get here?"

'Well, it was a nice problem, as you can understand, sir. We talked it over. First we thought of taking the machine away, leaving a letter for you to say what had happened. Then we saw that wouldn't do, because if we left the letter in a conspicuous place the other people would find it when they came, and know all about it. If we put the letter where they couldn't see it, you wouldn't know it was there. Anyway, after a lot of ideas that we didn't like, we decided that the only thing to do was to split up, him taking the machine to a safe place, and me staying here to tell you what had happened. So he took off, and it was a good thing he did, for he hadn't been gone many minutes when I heard a crowd coming. I shinned up a tree and watched.

'There must have been about twenty of them, all in uniform, and they kicked up a rare old row when they found the machine had gone; they could see where it had been, of course, by the wheel marks. The chap who seemed to be in charge went to the edge of the wood and stared up at the sky for about ten minutes; then he gave it up as a bad job I suppose, for he pushed off, leaving a couple of men on guard. Just before it got dark, a fellow came along on horseback and gave them fresh orders I fancy, for they all went away together. I wasn't sorry either, I can tell you, for I was getting pretty stiff up my tree. I hung about keeping watch, and I got back up the tree when I heard you coming, in case it wasn't you.'

'Yes, but where has Mr Lacey gone and what is he going to do?' asked Biggles impatiently. 'They're searching the forest for us now, and they'll comb it from end to end as soon as it is daylight. Quite apart from the machine, they know that two of us are here, anyway.'

'How?'

'They've seen us. I haven't time to tell you about it, but they're after us. We managed to give them the slip in the dark, but I doubt if we can hang out very long in daylight. What did Mr Lacey say he was going to do?'

'He said he'd push off to that small lake we passed on the way here, and stay there until morning. He's coming back as soon as it is daylight to pick us up at the northern extremity of this lake.'

'I suppose it was the best he could do in the circumstances, but this all sounds a crazy business to me. We hadn't very much petrol as it was, and if he goes tearing about the sky looking for somewhere to land, he'll run out altogether, and then we shall be in a nice mess. The idea of landing anywhere on this lake makes me go cold. With the whole crowd looking for us I don't see how it can be done without us being seen.'

'But he wasn't to know that,' put in Ginger. 'I don't see what else he could do.'

'No, I suppose you're right,' admitted Biggles, 'but I wish he'd arranged some other landing place.'

'I don't suppose he knew of one; he wouldn't be such a fool as to land on this very spot again, knowing that it was certain to be watched.'

'He didn't like the idea of coming down on land,' put in Smyth. 'He said, "If I run into a tree stump or something bang goes the whole works." That's why he decided to come down on water, which he reckoned was the only safe thing to do. At one time we thought of asking you to try and reach the other lake on foot.'

'Well, it's no use wondering what we might have done or should have done; we know what we have got to do, so let's do it. We'd better start working up towards the northern end of the lake.'

Crack! The whip-like report of a rifle shot, not very far away, made them all jump. It was followed by a shout, which in turn was followed by others.

'Yes, it's high time we were moving;' went on Biggles crisply, 'they're beating the forest for us, and they're shooting first and asking questions afterwards by the sound of it. Indian file, and take it slowly, but we must be in position by the time Algy lands. He won't be able to hang about waiting for us.'

With Biggles leading they set off towards the lake, and on reaching it turned towards the north, keeping the lake always in sight. It was a march that was to live in their memories for many a day. The moon came out from behind a cloud, and made things easier, but it flung curious shadows that often made them freeze into immobility until they were satisfied that the suspicious object was not a human being. Once, a water fowl rose up with a whirr of wings from under their feet, and brought their hearts into their mouths; but it served a useful purpose, for a voice spoke sharply from somewhere just ahead on their line of march. They just had time to crawl under some bushes and throw themselves flat when a crashing in the undergrowth warned them that someone was approaching. A moment later a man appeared at the water's edge, with a rifle held at the ready. He walked slowly towards them looking to right and left, and came to a stop not twenty yards away. Another voice called out from somewhere quite close, and the man answered, but they could not understand what he said. Shortly afterwards, to their infinite relief, he walked back in the direction from which he had come.

Ginger drew a deep breath. 'Say!' he breathed, 'this is giving me the heebie-jeebies; what are we going to do?'

'We're going on because it's no use going back,' muttered Biggles.

'The place is alive with people,' whispered Smyth.

'We can't help that. If anyone sees us we shall have to make a bolt for it; if they start shooting, I'll show them that two can play at that game. If I have to stop you two keep on and I'll follow as fast as I can.'

'I've got a gun, too,' whispered Ginger.

'You keep it in your pocket; I shall feel safer. I don't think you've any ammunition left, but I don't want the back of my head blown off in the dark,' Biggles told him curtly. 'Come on.'

Almost at once they came upon an open lane, or drive, that had been cut through the forest. Biggles held up his hand, dropped on all fours, and crawled towards it with infinite care. He moved his head forward towards the edge of the cutting, looked both ways quickly, and then rejoined the others. He caught Ginger by the wrist and pulled him down until his ear was level with his mouth. 'Two men – twenty yards away,' he breathed. He did the same to Smyth. 'Don't move an inch,' he warned them. 'Crack a twig now and we're done.'

'Follow the lane until we come to a turn, then we can cross,' suggested Ginger, in an almost inaudible whisper.

Biggles shook his head. 'No use,' he said. 'The lane runs straight down to the water; we can't cross without being seen. We must wait.'

They sat still, hardly daring to breathe, for what must have been half an hour, but it seemed like hours, and still the men showed no signs of moving. Biggles began to get anxious. 'We shall have to risk it,' he whispered at last. 'We daren't waste any more time. It's two or three miles to the end of the lake, and it will start getting daylight presently.'

'Let me try something,' suggested Ginger. 'I know a trick that may work. It's risky; that's why I haven't suggested it before. The second you hear a crash in the bushes dart across. Don't wait, it has to be done like lightning.' He took his automatic from his pocket by the muzzle, fondled it a moment regretfully, and then, before the others were aware of his intention, he stepped into an open space and hurled it far into the air in the direction of the sentries. For perhaps five seconds, long enough for Biggles and Smyth to think he had taken leave of his senses, there was silence, and then a crash of twigs, followed by a thud as the weapon fell to the ground well beyond the sentries.

The moment it had left his hand he had dropped into the position of a sprinter at a starting post, and the others, suddenly understanding, did the same. While the echoes of the crash were still in their ears, they darted across the open space to the black shadows beyond, and lay motionless wherever they happened to alight.

There came a muttered exclamation from the truck, and the sound of footsteps, running, footsteps that were obviously going farther away. There was a shout and an answering shout from the distance.

'OK,' said Ginger softly, 'they didn't see us. They were looking the other way – they wouldn't have been human if they hadn't.'

'Pretty good,' observed Biggles, 'but why didn't you do it before?'

'Too risky. There's always the chance of the stone, or gun, as it was in this case, hitting a branch or something and falling in the wrong place. If my gun had fallen *this* side of those fellows, instead of the other side, where should we have been?'

'It didn't, that's all that matters,' returned Biggles.

'We shall have to hurry now, keep close together. I shall be glad when we get there.'

'So shall I,' muttered Ginger. 'Crawling about in woods with keepers about is bad enough, but when you know that a gun might go off in your ear at any moment, it gets past a joke.'

'All right, that's enough. Quiet now.'

Like three shadows flitting across the silent aisles of the forest, they continued on their way, always keeping the lake in sight. Once, a large creature leapt up in front of them and threw them into a momentary panic. Biggles's revolver was out in a flash, but he dropped the muzzle when he saw it was an animal – deer or wild hog, it was gone too quickly for them to see. Ginger had clutched Biggles's arm in his alarm, and loosed it sheepishly as they went on.

'Getting nervous?' asked Biggles, nudging Smyth.

'Nervous! No, I'm not nervous. I'm so frightened that if we don't soon get to this place we're going to, my hair will be white, and you'll have to find another name for me.'

'We can't be far off now,' Biggles assured him. His words proved to be true, for a couple of minutes later the lake swung round in a wide arc towards the opposite bank.

'Yes, this is the end,' Biggles went on, after a quick survey. 'We'll work round the bank a bit towards the middle I think, and then we shall be in the dead centre of the northern end.'

The ground under their feet began to get swampy, and forced them to choose a path a little farther from the water.

'We shall have to choose a hiding place near a spot that is free from rushes, so that Algy can taxi right to

126

the shore and pick us up; we don't want to have to wade out and get wet through, besides, we shall have no time to lose,' observed Biggles. 'What's this ahead? It looks like the ideal spot. Yes, this will do; we shan't find a better place.'

The spot at which they had halted was at the foot of a fairly steep bank, as if rough water had at some time eaten into the land leaving an abrupt bank some five or six feet deep, from which the exposed roots of trees hung out like the tentacles of an octopus. 'There's nothing we can do now except wait,' he continued. 'It isn't worth while trying to sleep, as it should start getting light fairly soon; but if we don't soon find some food we shall be in a bad way.'

'You've said it,' agreed Ginger moodily, 'I've never been so short of grub in my life.'

Slowly the stars faded and the eastern sky began to turn from black to grey; water hens appeared on the water, and a dog began barking in the distance. Gradually the wan light grew stronger until it was light enough to see across the water to the seaplane station, about three miles away.

'He should be here any minute now,' said Biggles.

A strong wind blew up from the south and drove the water on the bank, in waves of increasing size, but they were not large enough to affect the Vandal's landing. An hour passed, and Biggles rose to his feet with a worried frown on his face.

'He's a long time coming,' he muttered.

The others did not answer. Ginger was chewing a grass stalk reflectively.

The sun rose higher and they were grateful for its warmth but still there was no sign of the Vandal. The morning wore on, but still it did not come, and Biggles suddenly faced the others squarely.

'Something's gone wrong,' he said shortly. 'If he was coming he would be here by now. It's no use pretending any longer; something has happened to him. Are you quite sure this was the place he meant Smyth?'

'I'm certain of it, sir.'

'This other lake – the one he was going to – isn't more than twenty miles away, is it?'

'Barely that I should think.'

'Well, we had better wait here a bit longer. Smyth, you watch the left bank and you keep an eye on the right, Ginger. I'll guard the rear. If either of you see anyone, let me know.'

Chapter 11
What Happened to Algy

Algy's troubles had begun almost immediately after his rush into the air to prevent the Vandal from falling into the hands of those he now classed as 'the enemy'. On the face of it, his plan seemed feasible enough, and so in ordinary circumstances it would have been; but the circumstances were far from ordinary. He knew, of course, that machines were out, watching for the British amphibian; that was obvious from the actions of those who had spotted it, but not until he was in the air did he realize how widespread was the hue and cry. He flew due west at first, flying back over the ground that the Vandal had covered on its way out, but the appearance of a machine on the horizon directly in front of him made him turn quickly. The wind, he noticed, had swung round to the south, and was bringing up a good deal of low cloud, a fact which did not please him, as he was by no means certain of the position of the small lake, and reduced visibility would not make the task of finding it any easier.

He kept a watchful eye on the solitary machine, and was presently relieved to see it disappear behind a mass of cloud, flying, as far as he could make out, on a course diagonally away from his own. He turned again to his original route, but had no sooner done so when a two-seater of military type emerged from a cloud not a mile away.

'Confound it,' he muttered irritably, as he dived

into the nearest cloud, wondering if he had been seen. He came out on the other side of it and once more began to veer round towards the lake. The country over which he was flying, being entirely new to him, furnished very little useful information, for there was an unusual dearth of roads and railways, and even buildings, a fact which tended to confirm Biggles's idea that they were actually in Russia.

He saw yet another machine, but it was a long way away, and with his old-time instinct he placed himself between it and the now sinking sun, knowing that in that position, it was highly improbable that he would be seen by the other pilot. 'My word,' he mused, 'we've stirred up a hornets' nest, and no mistake. This must be a pretty big thing if they have to turn out half the machines in Germany, or Russia, to look for us. We are going to have a bad time if we are caught, I can see that.' The increasing urgency for getting the machine hidden, and then getting out of the country as quickly as possible, was apparent, and still flying with as much caution as he did during the War, he nearly collided head-on with a machine that burst out of the cloud in which he himself proposed to take cover whilst approaching his objective.

Which of the two pilots was the more surprised it is impossible to say. Both banked vertically to the right, as international regulations demanded in such circumstances, and then levelled out. Algy did not stop to examine the details of the machine that had nearly rammed him; he shoved the stick forward and raced towards the wide belt of low cloud that stretched across the sky to the west. Visibility or no visibility, the lake became a matter of secondary consideration in the face of the new peril.

The other machine was much faster than the old Vandal, however, so the pilot overtook him rapidly and soon roared up alongside. Algy saw it was a two-seater, but it bore no registration marks of any sort; what interested him far more was the observer, who was standing up behind a wicked-looking machine gun. The gunner, seeing that Algy was watching him, held up his hand and beckoned, making it clear that he was to follow; as an alternative he pointed to his gun in a manner that left no doubt as to his meaning.

Now Algy had not the slightest desire to follow the other machine, but still less did he relish the idea of being shot to pieces by a modern quick-firing gun. Of the two evils he chose the lesser, and obediently altered his course to follow his captor, but he kept a watchful eye on the cloudbank, now over his left shoulder, determined to make a dash for it the moment an opportunity presented itself. If the worst came to the worst he would try and show the goggled figure in the front seat of the other plane a trick or two that he had acquired in the war skies of France. Meanwhile his brain was working with its old-time rapidity, although the situation was a new one. He pushed up his goggles and grinned at the other pilot, now not more than twenty yards away, but there was no answering smile.

'You miserable hound,' he thought, 'I should hate to serve in a squadron with a crowd of fellows like you.'

Straight ahead the cloudbank bulged out towards them, and he determined to make his attempt to escape as they passed it, for such an opportunity might not occur again; but the pilot of the other machine seemed to suspect his intention, for he began edging him farther away from the opaque mist.

'Oh dash this for a fool's game,' snarled Algy, suddenly losing his patience, and kicking out his left foot, jammed the stick forward and dragged it round to the left at the same time. The Vandal shot straight underneath its escort. Now Algy knew better than to run straight for the cloud, for he was aware that the gunner would have his weapon turned on him before he could get out of range, so using the speed he had accumulated in his dive, he pulled the stick back into his stomach and twisted up into the 'eye' of the sun.

For a moment the other pilot, unable to look in his direction without partially blinding himself, was at fault, as Algy hoped he would be, so seizing his chance, he pushed the stick forward and plunged down towards the cloud. The other saw him and gave chase immediately, but Algy's literally flying start had given him a lead of nearly a mile. Even so, it was touch and go, for once the other machine got into its stride it began to overtake him at an alarming rate, and bullets were whistling through the Vandal's planes as she roared down into the heart of the clammy moisture.

'Up, or down?' thought Algy, knowing that he could not hope to keep the machine on even keel for very long in such conditions without 'blind' flying instruments* – modern gadgets which Biggles disdained to use. 'Down,' he decided, and pressed gently on the stick. He found the ground about five hundred feet under the cloud, and after a swift glance around,

* A set of instruments to enable the pilot to fly straight and level in poor or nil visibility.

during which he put the machine on even keel, he zoomed up into the cloud again, pointing the nose of the Vandal in the direction of the lake.

If necessary he was prepared to land anywhere, but he had a horror of piling the Vandal up on a hidden obstruction, and he preferred the lake if he could find it. He held on his way for a while, dropping down from time to time to snatch quick glimpses of the terrain below, and presently saw a small wood which his practised eye recognized for one over which they had passed on their outward flight. It gave him his direction, and still skimming along in the gloom at the base of the cloud, he came suddenly upon that which he so anxiously sought, the small, wood-locked lake which they had passed that morning.

He snatched a swift look around, but could still see no sign of the other machine, so without further delay he put the Vandal down on the black water, sideslipping over the trees and keeping as close to the edge of the lake as the strong southerly wind would permit. Without waiting for the amphibian to finish its run, he opened the throttle again and charged at the nearest point of land that offered a fair amount of cover. The silver wings of the Vandal would, he knew, show up against the black water, like a white moth on a dark curtain, and give him away immediately should one of the searching machines happen to fly over.

He reached the bank at a swampy looking place that ran well under the dismal fir trees, with thick patches of reeds on either side, and dropping his wheels, he forced the machine up it as far as she would go. Then he switched off, and leaping down into several inches of greasy mud, began tearing up

133

armfuls of reeds and throwing them over his top plane and elevators. Not until the machine was literally covered – to say nothing of being well besprinkled with mud, did he desist, and throw himself wearily on the fir needles under the trees to rest.

It was nearly dark, and he became faintly aware that he was both tired and hungry. There was no point in keeping watch, he decided; if anyone came along he could do nothing about it now. 'If I try taking off from this black hole of Calcutta in the dark, I shall pile her up for certain,' he mused. 'And it's no use thinking about food; there isn't any, and that's that,' he concluded, so he tightened his belt and slithered back through the mud into the cabin, where presently, worn out after the day's excitement, he dropped off to sleep.

When he awoke he had no idea of the time, but he felt that it must be nearly morning, so in order that he should not drop off to sleep again, he sat up and waited for the dawn. In spite of his feeling that it was not far away, he found the waiting tedious, and he was heartily glad when at last the sky turned from black to grey. 'Thank goodness,' he muttered, 'now I'll see about getting off.' He crept through the hatchway into the cockpit and looked out; the sight that met his gaze stunned him almost as effectively as a blow would have done. During the night, the Vandal had sunk down into the soft mud until her keel was resting on the ooze; her wheels had completely disappeared.

For a moment or two his brain refused to act, so overcome was he at the calamity, for he knew that single-handed he could not hope to get her clear of the clinging slime. When the full horror of what he had done at last sank into his paralysed brain he nearly groaned aloud, and he sat back to try and collect his faculties, and think, if possible, of some manner in which the harm might be undone.

The fact that Biggles and the others were waiting for him at that very moment threw him into a frenzy, but it was of no avail, and by the time the sun was up he knew that he was helpless; the Vandal was anchored as securely as a lightship. He did not start the engine, knowing that it would be a sheer waste of time, besides running the risk of attracting the attention of foresters, or anyone who lived in the vicinity, who would no doubt report the presence of the aeroplane to the authorities.

The only thing he could hope for now, he decided, was that the others would guess that something tragic had happened to prevent his return, and would set off for the spot to which Smyth had no doubt told them he was going, on foot. He did the only thing he could do where the Vandal was concerned, and that was to collect fallen branches and thrust them down under the wheels to prevent the machine sinking any lower. He went as far as trying to dig the mud away from the wheels with his hands, and he did get one almost clear, but the ooze had seeped back again and filled up the hole before he could release the other.

Finally, plastered from head to foot with mud, he flung himself on the bank in utter dejection. Food was becoming a pressing question, and the lack of it aggravated his low spirits. He thought there might be fish in the lake, but he had no means of catching them. Slowly the most miserable day that he could ever remember came to an end, and faint from want of food he crept back into the cabin to wait for morning. He half regretted that he had not set out at once on foot for the larger lake, as soon as he discovered that the Vandal was out of action, but it had been the thought that Biggles might have already started towards the smaller lake that deterred him. If they passed each other on the way the position would simply be reversed and no good purpose served. At last, still racking his brains for a solution of the problem, he dropped off to sleep.

He was awakened by the reverberating roar of a low flying aeroplane, and with his heart in his mouth he hurried through to the cockpit and looked out. It was already daylight although the sun had not yet risen, but it was not that which sent his heart down into his boots. It was the aeroplane that Ginger had once so well described, a low-wing monoplane with a biplane tail – Blackbeard's seaplane. What was worse, the pilot had obviously seen the Vandal, for the seaplane made a quick turn, the engine was throttled back, and it began gliding down towards him with the plain intention of landing.

Algy watched its floats cut twin streaks of white foam across the black water, in silent misery.

Chapter 12
Trailed

The preceding day, twenty miles away, Biggles, Smyth and Ginger had spent an anxious day in their hiding place while the forest was being combed for them by an army of men, a fact which cries and the crashing of bushes did not allow them to forget. By the afternoon they had given up all hope of Algy's arrival, knowing that only dire catastrophe could have prevented him from arriving at the rendezvous at the appointed hour; so they concentrated their efforts on evading capture until such time as they could decide on a course of action. They had more than one narrow escape, for search parties came perilously close to them more than once. On one occasion, two men, carrying rifles, who had been beating the foreshore, actually started towards their place of concealment, but at the last moment their attention was distracted to a different quarter by a pair of wild ducks that arose into the air with loud quacks of alarm from some unseen cause.

With the approach of dusk the tension began to relax and they gathered together to discuss the position.

'This is how I see things,' began Biggles moodily. 'Algy is down somewhere with the machine. Whether he has force-landed and crashed, or whether the machine is still all right, we do not know, but it seems pretty certain that he is not in a position to fly the machine or he would be here. Whether shortage of petrol or engine failure is the cause does not matter; he isn't here and he can't get here by air. There is always a possibility that he landed safely, but was afterwards taken prisoner, and I am inclined to think that is what has happened, because if he himself was safe and sound he would get here somehow or other, even if he had to walk. That brings us to the crux of the problem with which we are faced. Assuming that he has managed to put the machine down some- where, and has damaged it so that he cannot get off again, I doubt if he would try and get here in broad daylight. With all the activity that has been going on he would be caught before he had gone a mile. I think it is far more likely, now I come to think of it, that he would wait for darkness and then try and reach us. He may be on his way here at this very moment.

'What is our position? Every moment we delay here is fraught with danger, yet as far as I can see we have no alternative but to remain. If we left, where should we go? There is only one place where we could hope to find him, and that is the other lake, but we have no reason to suppose that he ever reached it. Moreover, if we started now the odds are that we should pass each other in the dark. Bear in mind that we could not afford to hail, or even allow ourselves to be seen by any casual strangers we may meet, in the hope that it might be him. On the contrary, we should have to do our best to avoid such an encounter, for fear of it being one of the soldiers – or whatever they are.'

'There is just a chance, of course, that he may have had a temporary breakdown, something that he can repair himself, but it will take time,' suggested Smyth.

'In that case he's bound to come on here as soon as he can.'

'That's feasible,' admitted Biggles.

'The only thing you do not seem to have considered is this,' put in Ginger. 'What about those machines that made him leave here in the first place. Suppose he barged into them, what then? Even if they didn't shoot him down, which they might, they'd simply follow him until he landed, knowing that sooner or later he would have to come down for more petrol.'

'My word! I never thought of that,' muttered Biggles, his frown deepening. 'Lord, yes! That *would* put the tin hat on it.'

'Well, we can't help it,' went on Ginger, philosophically, 'if he had stayed here the result would have been the same.'

'It all boils down to this,' continued Biggles. 'The only thing we can do for the moment is to stay here in the hope that he will turn up somehow or other, but there is a limit to how long we can stay. Quite apart from the danger of being found, we can't go on without food much longer. If he isn't here by dawn tomorrow, we shall have to go. We'll make for the other lake, and if he isn't there, try to reach a railway and go to Danzig. The only thing we could do then would be to report the matter to the British Consul. After all, our papers are in order, and if questions were asked as to what we were doing here, who is to say that we did not simply lose our way or get blown off our course by bad weather? I'm beginning to wish that we had left this affair to the right people.'

'I guess you're right,' agreed Ginger, 'but we won't give up hope yet. Something will turn up, you'll find;

it usually does when things look as bad as they can be.'

'I hope you're right,' replied Biggles. 'I don't know about you, but it's taking me all my time to keep awake. It seems weeks since I slept or had a square meal. We've got to spend the night here, so I suggest we take watches in turn while the others sleep; if we don't get some sleep we shall be dead on our feet to-morrow. Ginger, you're all in, I can see. Lie down and try to get a nap – you do the same, Smyth. I'll take the first watch. You'll take the second watch, Smyth; I'll wake you in three hours, as near as I can judge. You do three hours and then wake Ginger. If anyone hears anything suspicious he will wake up the others at once.'

It seemed to Ginger that he had only just closed his eyes when he was awakened by a slight pressure on his shoulder. Accustomed to sleeping in strange places, often under the stars, he had dropped off to sleep as soon as his head touched the ground, and for the same reason he awoke just as easily.

'S-s-h! Don't make a noise,' came Smyth's voice, 'it's your watch, take over.'

'OK,' muttered Ginger, with a glance at Biggles's sleeping form.

The moon was up and cast an eerie light over the scene as he rubbed the sleep from his eyes and began his vigil. All was quiet in the forest except for the soughing of the wind in the trees and the lap of water on the beach, which was now littered with small pieces of squared timber and fabric that had either drifted down, or been blown before the wind from the work-shops. He gazed far across the rippling moonlit waters of the lake in the direction of the seaplane base, but no lights were showing. 'There,' he reflected, 'is food in abundance.' The thought prompted, no doubt, by the gnawing pain under his belt, persisted, and he regarded the distant shore meditatively. The thought quickly grew to a longing that was not to be denied.

For ten days, up to the time Biggles had found him in the railway hut, he had lived by 'scrounging,' as he called it, and he had acquired a good deal of experience in the ·art. 'I can't help them very much by staying here,' he mused, 'in fact, I'm really only in the way. If I *could* get hold of some grub I should feel that I was earning my keep.' His conscience pricked him over the matter of leaving the others without a guard, but they were sleeping quietly and the search parties seemed to have been withdrawn; a long time had elapsed since they had heard the last calls in the forest. Perhaps, if he was lucky, he could get back before they awoke. He had a pencil and an old notebook in his pocket; he would leave them a note, telling them of his project, in case he was delayed or did not return. What a treat it would give them to wake up and find food set before them!

The thought decided him, and he rose stealthily to his feet. The gloomy blackness of the forest rather appalled him; what wild beasts did it harbour? He thrust the thought aside, and, after a last glance at the sleeping figures of his companions, crept silently away. The sombre fir trees closed in around him, and he was alone in the forest.

Biggles awoke with a start, feeling that something was amiss, and sprang to his feet. He glanced down at the sleeping figure of Smyth, and then looked quickly to right and left.

'Ginger!' he said sharply.

There was no reply, but the sound awoke Smyth, who sat up abruptly.

'Where's that lad?' asked Biggles, looking down at him.

'Why, isn't he here?'

'I can't see him.'

'I left him on guard when I turned in.'

'Then what the dickens is he up to; scouting, I suppose, the young ass. Ginger!' he called again, but there was no answering hail.

'The young fool! I'll clip his ear when he comes back – hullo, what's this?' A small square of white paper had fluttered from his chest to the ground. He picked it up and saw that it was a leaf torn from a small notebook, and holding it up to the now fading moonlight, saw that there was writing on one side. 'This looks like a note,' Biggles went on. 'Hold your coat round me while I strike a match.'

'Dere Biggles,' he read, 'I've gon for some grubb. If I am not back by one houre after daylite go without me. Ginger.'

Biggles blew out the match and ground the spark under his heel.

'What d'you know about that, eh?' asked Smyth.

Biggles shrugged his shoulders helplessly. 'I don't know what to think about it,' he said despairingly. 'It's what in the old days would be called "acting on one's own initiative." It's the sort of mad thing that if it comes off makes the fellow a hero and gets him a decoration. If he fails he gets court-martialled and reprimanded for acting without orders. You can't help admiring the kid's pluck; it's the last thing I should have thought of doing, I must admit. Where on earth does he think he's going to get grub from about here? Surely he wouldn't be so absolutely crazy as to go back into the town.'

'That's where he's gone,' muttered Smyth, 'you can bet your life on that; there's nowhere else for him go to.'

'Well, God knows we need food badly enough, and if he manages to get some it would be unfair to blame him for going; but this scattering up of the party all over Russia is wrong, and the sooner we all get together again the better. I wish he hadn't gone; what are we going to do if he doesn't come back? We can't leave him here. I'll give him a ticking off about leaving his post, you may be sure of that, but I shall be relieved to see the young beggar back here. If anything happens to him – but there, it's no use worrying. I wonder what the time is.'

'Pretty nearly morning I should think, by the look of the sky. It will be light in another half-hour.'

'I wonder if they will think we have escaped or if they will go on searching again as soon as it is light?' mused Biggles.

As if in answer, a sound reached them that made Smyth clutch at Biggles' arm, and even he turned pale. It was the deep, long-drawn howl of a hound on a blood-scent.

'My God!' breathed Biggles, 'they've put hounds on our trail.'

Again the dreadful sound was borne on the breeze to their straining ears. In the dim light of the false dawn it seemed to hold a quality of sinister finality that turned their blood to ice.

'I remember that animal,' muttered Biggles. 'I heard it when I was walking along the railway track. Well, there's only one thing to do. God help that poor kid; we can't.'

'What shall we do?'

'Get into the water – wade out into the rushes. We'll try to work our way round to the other side. It's no use trying to hide now; that beast will bring the guards straight here. Come on.'

Side by side they waded out into the cold water and started off along the edge of the lake, but Biggles realized at once that the task was almost hopeless. Under the water, the mud was several inches deep, and this, combined with the tangled roots of rushes and water weeds, made progress well-nigh impossible.

'It's no use, Smyth,' said Biggles quietly, 'we shall never get anywhere at this rate.'

But Smyth was not listening. He was staring out over the water of the lake, now pale grey with the approach of dawn, at a dark object that seemed to be drifting towards them.

'It's a machine,' said Biggles in a strangled voice – 'Blackbeard's machine; I'd know it anywhere. This looks like the end.'

'No!' cried Smyth suddenly. 'The prop's stationary. It's adrift.'

There is an old saying that the darkest hour comes before the dawn, and never was it more graphically demonstrated. From hopeless despair their emotions swung round in a flash to joy and hope. If they could only reach the machine, the whole business would assume a very different aspect.

'What's that on the port float?' cried Biggles sharply.

'It looks to me as if it's somebody on that float,' replied Smyth in a queer voice, peering forward. 'It's hard to see, but it looks like somebody splashing.'

'It's too small for a man. My God, it's Ginger!' burst out Biggles, suddenly understanding. 'He must have cut it adrift, and the wind has blown him across. He's brilliant is that boy! That isn't cleverness, it's genius – genius,' he repeated in his enthusiasm. 'Look! He's trying to keep her straight with that piece of plank. Let's give him a hail so that he'll know we've seen him.'

The voice of the hound echoed weirdly through the trees not far away, and there was a crashing in the undergrowth.

'Hi, Ginger!' cried Biggles. 'Good boy – keep going!'

There was an answering wave from Ginger, whom they could now see was sitting astride a float, with his feet dangling in the water, wielding a piece of wood like a paddle. He had little control over the machine, however, which was drifting sideways before the wind at a good speed; he would have been powerless, of course, to travel in any other direction.

He was still fifty yards away from them when the deep bay of the hound burst out so close that Biggles turned, whipping out his revolver. Ginger must have heard it, too, for he redoubled his efforts to hasten the progress of the machine.

'This is going to be touch and go, Smyth,' said Biggles quietly, cool and alert now that the prospect of action was so close. 'Stand fast; we must avoid getting wet through if we can prevent it. As soon as the machine gets within reach, get to the prop. When she starts, get into the cabin as quickly as you can and

145

get Ginger in with you, he must be frozen stiff with cold.'

The crashing in the bushes was now right upon them, and the hound broke cover at the spot where they themselves the previous evening had struck the lake. A shot rang out and several men appeared at the edge of the forest just as Biggles grabbed the toe of the nearest float and swung the machine round. 'Hang on, Ginger!' he yelled, seeing that the boy was nearly exhausted, and sprang up into the cockpit. He fumbled with the unusual controls for a moment, but found the petrol cock and turned it on. 'Petrol on – switches off – suck in!' he shouted. 'Keep your heads, everybody!'

'Suck in!' roared Smyth, and pulled the propeller round three or four times, finishing with it nicely balanced on contact.

A rifle cracked and the bullet ricocheted off the engine cowling with a shrill *whang*.

'Contact!' yelled Smyth.

'Contact!' echoed Biggles.

The engine started with a bellow that awoke the sleeping echoes, and drowned the reports of the weapons on the bank. Smyth staggered, caught himself, and then scrambled into the little cabin beside Ginger, who had been right in his guess that the machine was a three-seater. The cabin was very much like that of a Puss-Moth*, the pilot sitting in front, with two passengers side by side behind.

Biggles saw Smyth stagger and knew that he had been hit, but he dare not wait to investigate. With rudder hard over he roared round in a whirlpool of

* British De Havilland high wing monoplane of the 1930s.

146

foam, and as the nose of the machine pointed towards open water, jerked the throttle wide open and skimmed across the surface of the lake. He took her off as soon as he dared, for bullets were now cutting long, vicious-looking wheals in the water around them, and zooming over the tree-tops, turned his nose towards the west. Only when he had put her on an even keel, and set his course to his satisfaction, did he turn to see how badly Smyth was hurt; but the mechanic made a deprecating gesture as he pointed to his shoulder, indicating that the bullet had only grazed him, so Biggles turned again to his task of flying the machine.

Presently he felt someone nudge him in the back, and half turning, saw Ginger offering him a good-sized hunk of bread and an onion. He took them with a sign of surprise and thanks, and with the stick in one hand and his breakfast in the other, headed for the smaller lake. The food was primitive in its simplicity, but he could not remember enjoying a meal so much. It put new life into him, and with his old self assurance reasserting itself, he looked around the sky for possible enemies. He did not see another machine, however, during the ten minutes it took him to reach the lake. He circled it once, looking for the Vandal, and at last, to his great relief, picked it out in spite of its protective covering of weeds and rushes.

He landed and saw Algy watching him morosely, but as he taxied towards him, he saw him jump down on to the bank and run towards the wood. Not until then did Biggles remember that Algy had no means of knowing who was in the machine, so he raced tail up towards the Vandal, switching off only at the last moment. 'Get out and stop him, Ginger,' he snapped, 'or we shall lose him again.'

'Hi, Algy!' shouted Ginger, as he leapt down into the mud.

Algy heard him at once, and the expression of comical amazement on his face as he turned set them all laughing.

'What the – who the – where the—' he stammered.

'We'll tell you about it later; we've got to move quickly now,' replied Biggles. 'What's wrong with the Vandal?'

'Nothing except that she is bogged.'

'Thank goodness. That's why you didn't come back?'

'Of course.'

'Is she in very deep?'

'Not so far that the four of us can't get her out, I think, but I couldn't do it single-handed.'

'Let's have a look at her. Smyth, take a look and see how much petrol there is in the tanks of this machine. If we can get the Vandal clear we'll transfer it.'

It took them an hour, working like Trojans, to get the Vandal clear of her slimy bed, and they all breathed more freely as she floated out on to the water, filthier than she had ever been in all her travels. It took them another twenty minutes to transfer the petrol. The tanks were not so full as they had hoped, but they contained a fair amount, which augmented the Vandal's now very scanty supply.

Somewhat to their surprise, but to their great relief, they were not molested, although more than once they heard the drone of an aero-engine in the distance; but it was not until they were all on board the Vandal, with Algy munching a dry crust ravenously, that they began to feel really safe.

'Which way are you going?' he asked, as they waited for the engine to warm up.

'I'm going to make for Sweden,' replied Biggles. 'I want to get out of this country as soon as I can, and we should be mad to try and fly back over Germany. We should be seen and stopped before we had gone ten miles. I'll warrant every policeman in the country is on the look-out for us, and the first town we pass over will set the telephones ringing; it's a case of any port in a storm, and Sweden is the nearest. I don't think they dare touch us there. Once we strike the coast, we'll cruise down it until we come to a town where we'll fill up with petrol and push on for home. Where's that case you had, Ginger?'

'I threw it away, but the papers are in my pocket.'

'Good. I'm anxious to hear how you managed to steal an aeroplane, but we shall have to postpone that story until we get somewhere where there is no risk of being blown up or shot down.'

He pushed the throttle open and the Vandal soared into the air like a bird.

Chapter 13
Fog

They began their long flight with a good deal of trepidation, but as the time passed and they saw no signs of pursuit, the tension which they all felt became less severe and they looked forward to reaching their destination without being molested. With less petrol in the tanks than he would have liked, Biggles could not afford to make detours round frontiers, so he flew in a straight line, keeping slightly to the east of north-east. He could only vaguely guess when he had passed the Soviet boundary, although he had his map open beside him, but when he thought he had done so, he turned a trifle more to the north to avoid East Prussia; even so, it was necessary to make a dash across the most northerly part of it, for to have gone right up to Lithuania, and then flown due east towards Sweden, as he would have liked to have done, would have meant taking a dangerous risk with their scanty supply of petrol, particularly in view of the long sea passage before them when they reached the Baltic.

They saw two or three machines in the far distance as the sea came into sight, but the pilots were either not concerned with them or did not see them, for they made no move in the direction of the amphibian. The front main tank gave out just as they reached the coast, and Biggles switched over to the rear tank with a grimace at Algy, for he would have liked to have done better. The smoke of a steamer attracted his attention, and he saw with a shock that the wind, which had so opportunely blown Ginger across the lake when he had purloined Blackbeard's machine, had now swung right round in the opposite direction, and was directly in their teeth. This at once reduced their chances of reaching Sweden with a reasonable margin of fuel, but there was no help for it; they could only keep on.

The land faded away behind them, but they did not abandon their vigilance, knowing that both German and Russian sea and air craft operate over the Baltic, and there was still a chance that if the passage of the Vandal had been seen by watchers on the ground, a wireless message might send a machine, or machines, to intercept them. But as the day wore on into the afternoon, and still no aeroplanes were sighted, they began to congratulate themselves on their escape, and look joyfully ahead for land, which could only be Sweden, their objective. An exclamation of satisfaction escaped Biggles's lips when at last it appeared on the horizon.

'We've made it!' he shouted to Algy, and at that very moment the second tank failed. He switched over at once to the gravity tank, which contained about enough spirit to keep them in the air for another twenty minutes. 'I spoke too soon,' he went on grimly; 'it's going to be a close thing. If we can hold on long enough to get our wheels on Swedish soil, I don't mind.'

The coastline became more clearly defined, but they seemed to approach it with exasperating slowness, and all the time the precious petrol was being rapidly burnt up in the cylinders. Suddenly the engine coughed, spluttered and died away; the prop stopped, and the nose of the Vandal tilted down.

Biggles glanced at his altimeter and saw that the needle hovered on the five thousand mark. The shore was still a good five miles away. 'Can't do it,' he said calmly in the uncanny silence.

'We can—just,' contradicted Algy.

'We might if we were alone; we're four up, remember. We shall be about a quarter of a mile short. Still, if we can hit a town we shall be seen, and a boat will no doubt tow us in. Can you see a town anywhere—I can't.'

'Nor I,' replied Algy, 'I don't see a sign of life anywhere.'

'That's a pity,' answered Biggles, 'but we're lucky there isn't a big sea running, anyway. If the tide is right for us we may drift ashore; it looks low and sandy, thank goodness.'

He proved to be correct in his estimate as to how far the Vandal would glide with her heavy load, for she nosed down gently, and by holding her off as long as he could, Biggles at last touched the keel on the water about two or three hundred yards from the flat, sandy foreshore. 'So near and yet so far,' he muttered tritely. 'It seems silly to fail by such a narrow margin after coming so far, but we did our best. One would have thought there would have been a house of some sort about, even if it were only a fisherman's hut, but I can't see a blessed thing. I wonder which way the tide is running?'

'It's hard to tell,' replied Algy, climbing out of the cockpit to the top of the hull, where the other three joined him. 'Let's watch for a bit,' he suggested.

Half an hour later they were no nearer the shore,

but they were some distance from the place where they had first landed, and it became clear that they were being carried down the coast, on a course parallel with it, by a strong current.

'We shall come to a village or something presently,' announced Algy confidently.

'I hope you're right. We shall soon have to start doing something.'

'Why—what do you mean?'

'Look at the sun!'

The others turned their eyes towards where the sun now glowed redly in the west.

'It's going to do something presently,' went on Biggles, 'but I am not quite sure what. That sun either means fog or wind.'

The others made no reply, but sat and watched the sun being slowly blotted out by a rapidly thickening haze. The horizon disappeared.

'Hark!' As Biggles spoke, he sprang to his feet, staring seaward. 'There they are, three of them,' he muttered tersely.

The others, following his outstretched arm, saw three tiny black specks against the grey sky, three specks that grew rapidly larger even as they watched.

'Probably Swedish Air Force machines,' said Algy. 'They go in for seaplanes quite a lot.'

'I hope you're right, but I am afraid you're wrong,' Biggles told him calmly. 'I don't like the way they just changed their direction. They were heading pretty well due east a moment ago, and then it almost seemed as if they had spotted us by the way they turned. Yes,' he went on after a moment's pause, 'that settles it; that's Blackbeard's machine in front; there's no mistaking it. Hi! Where are you going?'

The last remark was addressed to Ginger, who had swung one leg over the side of the Vandal.

'We'd better swim for it, hadn't we?'

'Don't be a young fool; come back. Look at the rate we're drifting. How much headway do you think you'd make against that five-knot current? Come back here. Stand fast, everybody.'

There was no longer any doubt about either the identity or intentions of the pilots of the three seaplanes, for their engines were cut off and they began to glide down towards the helpless amphibian. At the last moment, either by pre-arrangement, or in obedience to a signal made by Blackbeard, who was leading, the two rear machines opened up their engines again and began circling, evidently in order to act as escort to the third machine which was now surging through the water at the end of its landing run.

A curious expression crept over Biggles' face as Blackbeard's seaplane, now swinging round in a wide turn towards them, suddenly assumed a dim, ghostly appearance. 'The fog!' he cried excitedly, 'the fog—it's coming down!'

Blackbeard seemed to realize it, too, for his machine yawed violently as he tried to bring it round too quickly; but he was too late. The outline of the seaplane became a vague, grey shadow that merged swiftly into the mist until it was lost to view. A moment later, curling fingers of white mist reached out towards the Vandal's wing-tips, filtered through the bracing wires, and then enfolded the whole machine in its clammy embrace.

For a full minute the four watchers on the Vandal stood staring stupidly into the grey pall, and then with

154

one accord they turned towards each other. The roar of the engines of the two machines overhead made conversation almost impossible, but presently the noise began to recede, and Biggles grinned derisively. 'They're climbing out of it–and so should I,' he observed. 'This is about the rummiest state of affairs I ever struck in my life. What I should really like to know is, is Blackbeard still on the water, or did he take off again when he saw what was happening? I had an idea that he opened his throttle again at the last moment, but the other two machines were making such a row that I couldn't be sure.'

'Yes, he opened up again,' declared Smyth, 'but I think that was in order to try and reach us before the fog blotted us out. I don't think he took off.'

'Stand still, let's listen,' said Biggles.

They stood silent for a little while, but the only sound that reached them was the fast-diminishing drone of the machines in the air, but whether there were two or three of them it was impossible to say.

'Everybody keep his eyes skinned,' ordered Biggles sharply. 'If Blackbeard is on the water, we don't want him barging into us in this murk. I wonder how he got his machine back? Somebody must have seen it on the lake after we left, I expect, and somebody else told the authorities the direction we were taking. Could anybody see how many people there were in the cabin?'

'Two, I think,' put in Ginger. 'I saw a face looking at us out of the side cabin window, and I thought there was another face behind, but I couldn't be quite sure.'

'All right, but we must be quiet. Sound carries a long way in this atmosphere.'

'What had we better do?' inquired Algy.

'Can you think of anything to do?' asked Biggles inquiringly.

'No, I can't, and that's a fact.'

'Neither can I except sit here and wait until something happens. It seems to me that everything depends on what occurs between now and when the fog lifts, although personally I don't think it will lift this side of nightfall; it's a typical evening fog caused by a change of temperature following evaporation during the heat of the day. We were lucky; it came in the nick of time, but it's a bit worrying. We were drifting at a good rate when it came down, and daylight might find us out of sight of land; on the other hand, we might drift ashore during the night.'

'Pity we couldn't have made that last two hundred yards,' muttered Ginger regretfully. 'I wonder—'

'Listen, my lad,' interrupted Biggles quietly, 'never worry your head wondering what *might* have happened–that doesn't matter two hoots. Always stick to facts; they are the only things that count. We *didn't* reach the coast, so all the wondering in the world about what might have happened if we had is a sheer waste of time. Remember that.'

'OK chief,' replied Ginger obediently.

'Well, it will soon be getting dark by the look of it,' went on Biggles, 'so some of us might as well see about taking a rest. We'll keep watches as before, two on duty and two off. If Blackbeard's machine is on the water we may drift together, so keep a good lookout. If we do collide, we'll try and fend him off; we'll avoid trouble as long as we can.'

Chapter 14
Blackbeard Speaks

It was pitch dark when Biggles, whose turn it was to rest, was awakened by Ginger shaking his shoulder. 'What is it?' he asked quickly.

'We're drifting ashore.'

'Are you certain?'

'Positive. I can hear waves lapping.'

Biggles hurried through to the cockpit just as the machine gave a lurch and remained tilted on its side. 'You're right,' he said softly, 'we're aground. What's about the time?'

'I don't know, but it must be getting on towards daylight,' answered Smyth, who was keeping watch with Ginger.

'I see; wake up Mr Lacey, one of you, will you?' Biggles climbed over the side and found he could stand in about two feet of water. The fog was, if anything, more dense than ever, and in the darkness it was impossible to see a yard.

'What about it?' asked Algy, joining him.

Biggles drew a deep breath and shook his head doubtfully. 'God knows,' he said, 'this has got me baffled. We may be on the mainland and we may be on an island; we may be just aground in shoal water. We daren't risk leaving the machine; we should never find it again in this muck, and if we happen to be on a sandbank we should be in a mess. I don't think anybody could go five yards in this without losing all sense of direction. The machine might even drift away and leave us stranded if we left her. I don't even know whether the tide is going in or out, so inside ten minutes the machine may be either afloat again, or high and dry.'

'Someone might stay with the machine and keep in touch with the others by shouting.'

'Useless! It's hopeless to try and locate a sound in this sort of stuff; one moment it seems to come from one direction and the next from somewhere else. We can't afford to lose the Vandal. I'm afraid we shall have to sit tight until the fog lifts. How long is our anchor line? We might tie someone on to the end of it and let him do a bit of exploring.'

'About fifty or sixty feet.'

'Get it out, will you.'

'I'll do the exploring,' suggested Ginger.

'No, you don't, my lad, not this time. Tie the rope round your waist, Algy, and we'll pay it out from here. You give a tug when you want to come back—we'd better not do any shouting. Go straight ahead and try to find out if we're on the shore. If we are, we've nothing to fear from Blackbeard, because we could make a bolt for it if it came to the worst, although I should be sorry to have to leave the machine.'

Algy tied the rope to his belt and disappeared into the darkness on the shallow side of the machine. He remained away for so long without any sort of signal that the others began to get anxious, for the line was out at its full length. At last the expected tug came, and he reappeared, soaked to the skin, and his teeth chattered with cold. 'I can't make it out,' he said as he scrambled aboard. 'There's dry sand a few yards ahead, but I can hear water on the other side. I'm

158

afraid it's a sandbank. I went up to the right afterwards, as far as the line would permit, and I heard
someone talking. It sounded like two or three people
having an argument.'

'How far away?' asked Biggles quickly.

'It's impossible to say, but not more than a hundred
yards at the outside, I should think. The fog, when
you are out in it, is simply appalling. I got so giddy
that I fell down two or three times.'

'That's Blackbeard, and if you could hear them,
then they've probably heard us.'

'I don't think so. What little breeze there is is blowing this way, and we've kept our voices fairly low.'

'Great Scot' muttered Biggles irritably, 'I shall go
crazy before this trip is over. I've been in some funny
jams, but I've never seen anything so absolutely foot-
ling as this. I've been lost before, but this is about the
limit. You say you could hear water the other side of
the sand?'

'It sounded like it to me.'

'Then we must be on a sandbank.'

'I'm afraid you're right, but why take it for granted
that the voices are those of Blackbeard and his passengers?'

'Because it stands to reason that we should drift at
the same rate. The machines weren't a hundred yards
apart when the mist blotted us out. If Blackbeard shut
off his engine for fear of colliding with us, as he
probably would for fear of smashing his prop, we
should both drift along at the same rate and come
ashore pretty well at the same spot.'

'Yes, I suppose we should,' admitted Algy, 'but if
that is the case they must be as helpless as we are.'

'Of course they are. They've got an engine, but it

159

isn't much use to them, and it won't be until the fog lifts. They couldn't hope to find us in this stuff, and there would be a good chance of them getting out of the locality altogether. They are bound to wait until it gets light before they do anything.'

'In which case we shall be in a nasty mess. They'll shoot us up with their machine-gun,' muttered Ginger.

'Machine-gun!'

'Yes, didn't you see it; the fellow in the cabin shoved it through the window just as the fog came.'

'That puts a different complexion on matters,' said Biggles slowly. 'I see the idea now. I was wondering how they proposed to take us back with them if they did catch us, but, of course, it would be easier to sink us. We might have expected it. They wouldn't have bothered to have followed us if they hadn't decided on drastic action. Unfortunately they must know we are out of petrol, too, or have had a breakdown, otherwise we shouldn't have landed where we did. It will be interesting to see what happens when the curtain goes up.'

'Did you say interesting?' asked Ginger incredulously. 'Sitting here and being shot by two Huns with a machine-gun isn't my idea of an interesting performance. Why stay here, anyway. Why not attack them now while they are unprepared?'

Biggles smiled. 'That sort of thing may be all right in books,' he said, 'but it doesn't work in real life. This is nineteen thirty-four. What on earth should we do with them if we caught them? Kill them? That's murder. No, we can't do that, and we can't take prisoners, even supposing we had that opportunity. On the other hand, if they happened to be wide awake, and met us with a tune out of their gun, we should look pretty foolish. Suppose we found that we couldn't reach them after all, and then found that we'd lost the Vandal, what four silly asses we should look in the morning marooned on a sandbank with the tide coming in.'

'I wasn't thinking of anything so daft as leaving the Vandal,' answered Ginger. 'We could take her with us.'

'That's an idea,' agreed Biggles quickly, 'but this attack scheme is no use. All the same, we might try towing the machine in the other direction, keeping in shallow water. If we find it runs deep, we can climb aboard and let her drift, although there would be a risk of being blown out to sea, but the farther we get from our Boche friends before daylight, the happier I shall feel. Well, if we're going to try it, we may as well make a start, or it won't be worth while; it seems to be getting grey already, so it can't be far off morning. Towing a flying boat through this stuff without knowing where we are or where we are going, is just about the maddest thing I ever heard of, but it's better than doing nothing. Come on, get that rope over her nose. She's only just resting on the sand, so we can easily haul her off.'

The task of towing the Vandal proved to be more awkward than fatiguing. Once afloat, she moved easily through the water, but without a visible mark to guide them, they often floundered into deep water as the machine swung from side to side at the slightest uneven pressure on the tow rope. Gradually the mist turned from grey to white, but still it showed no signs of lifting, so it was impossible for them to judge the progress they were making or how far they had travelled. From time to time they halted, while one or the other tested the depth of the water on either side, but the sandbank seemed to run on for ever.

'I may be mistaken, but I'm beginning to feel that we're going round in circles,' panted Algy at last. 'I suppose it isn't possible for us to work our way right round this sandbank or island, or whatever it is, and barge into Blackbeard's machine from the other side.'

'My word! I should think there is a jolly good chance of it,' muttered Biggles. 'It's easy enough to travel in circles in a fog like this. I'm getting perished, anyway, so let's lay up for a bit. We must have travelled quite a distance, although whether we've got farther out to sea or nearer to shore is more than I can say. I think it's getting lighter now–well I'm—!'

With a suddenness that seemed impossible, the great fog belt had lifted. It was almost as if an unseen hand had raised the curtain of a mighty stage, exposing the scene that lay beyond it. The effect was stupefying, and for a full minute all four of them remained rooted to the ground in sheer astonishment whilst the Vandal floated lazily towards them under the impetus of the last pull on the rope. Biggles began to laugh, and the others joined in as the strain of their vigil ended abruptly and the humour of the situation struck them. They laughed and laughed again until Biggles leaned against the hull and sobbed.

'That's enough,' he pleaded at last. 'Well, I've done some fool tricks in my life, but this is about the frozen limit. It just shows what you can do in a fog.'

There was a good reason for their humour, for they all stood in the middle of a narrow river up which they had been towing the Vandal. Within thirty yards of them on either side were the banks, one steep and thickly wooded, but the other fairly open, although dotted here and there with stunted pine trees. About a mile behind them, in the direction from which they had come, the river widened into an estuary that opened out into the open sea, now ruffled by the slight breeze that blew away the last vestiges of the mist, and left only the blue sky above them from which the sun shone brightly.

In the clear light of day it was easy to see what had happened. They had struck the sand-bar, such as one so often finds at the mouths of rivers, just beyond the estuary, and following it blindly, had dragged the Vandal up the river itself. As a matter of fact, the sand-bank actually ended a few yards farther on, so had they persisted in their efforts, they would have struck deep water, and climbing aboard, drifted back to the sea.

There was no one in sight, not a house, or any sign of human habitation; nor could they see Blackbeard's seaplane.

'Wade across to the bank and take a look out to sea, Ginger,' said Biggles.

Ginger obediently splashed his way through the shallow water, and scrambled up the sand dune that formed the bank on the open side. Near the top he dropped on all fours and peeped over. Simultaneously, the roar of an aeroplane engine shattered the silence from somewhere near at hand, the sound coming from a point so close that they all started and rushed towards the Vandal in confusion. Ginger took one peep and then tore back to the machine. His eyes were round with wonderment when he reached it, and for a moment he seemed to have some difficulty in speaking.

'How far away is it?' asked Biggles.

'It! Not so much of the "it," ' gasped Ginger. 'There are two of 'em. Blackbeard's machine is one, and the other—'

'Go on.'

'It's one of the giant bombers, and there's a crowd of people aboard.'

'What!' Biggles sprang round as if he had been stung.

'It's a fact, and it isn't more than a mile away. Blackbeard has just started his engine, and he's only just on the other side of the hill. The sea comes right in again round the corner.'

'But how on earth did the big machine get here without us hearing it?' exclaimed Algy.

'I should say one of the other machines called it up by radio as soon as we were spotted, and we didn't hear it coming for the noise of the other machines. The fog forced it down, no doubt, and it drifted in on the same current as ourselves. The thing is, what are we going to do about it? We can't hide the Vandal, and they'll spot it the moment they take off. I think our best plan is to moor up to the bank and then make for the nearest town. For the life of me, I can't see what the Huns can do now. After all, we're in Sweden, and they can't kick up a rumpus here without the authorities taking a hand. But let's get ashore.'

It was the work of a moment to pull the Vandal to the far bank and tie her securely to the nearest tree.

'Are we going to leave somebody with the machine?' asked Algy.

'Not on your life,' retorted Biggles. 'They're not interested in the machine; it's us they want. The machine can't tell tales--we can. Anybody they get hold of will go back to Russia in the big machine; that's probably why they brought it. No! Safety first is the motto. We stick together this time; the machine will have to take care of itself–look out!'

The crescendo bellow of Blackbeard's engine warned them that he was about to take off, and they ran up the slope into the wood just as the seaplane zoomed over the opposite bank. The pilot saw them– or it may have been that he saw the Vandal only– instantly, for he banked sharply and then circled above the spot. Then he straightened out and, heading off in a straight course over the wooded hill, disappeared from sight.

'Now what's his game, I wonder?' murmured Biggles from the cover of the trees. 'Where's he off to? No matter, let us push on and try to find a village of some sort. I cannot see that he can do any mischief now, but you never know,' he went on as they breasted the steep, timber-covered slope, and then stopped dead as the landscape beyond came into view. In front of them, but slightly below and about two miles away, were the outskirts of a large seaport town. The streets were thronged with traffic, and a fleet of small boats, with one or two large deep-sea craft amongst them, were at anchor in the harbour.

'Well, there's our destination,' he continued, 'although I hardly expected to find such a big place so handy. Hullo! There's Blackbeard's machine just taxi-ing in; it will be interesting to see what his next move will be, although I have a nasty feeling that he has something up his sleeve. All the same, if we can get petrol here, I don't see why we shouldn't ask for police protection if necessary. It might be difficult to get away while he is hanging about here with that gun—but let us take one thing at a time; we'll deal with that difficulty when it arrives. A square meal is the first thing we want; if I don't soon get some food I shall pass out. After that we'll see about the petrol.'

'You've sure said it,' declared Ginger emphatically.

'Come on, then, let's go and see about it,' returned Biggles, starting forward.

They soon struck a road, and, following it in the direction of the town, came out about half an hour later on the waterfront near the harbour. It was with mingled relief and curiosity that they once more mixed with the sights and sounds of civilization, but they did not pause to enjoy them; they were all far too hungry. They hurried along the street, and although they were rather self-conscious of their untidy condition, they attracted no attention.

Biggles turned into the first restaurant they reached and seated himself at a table with a smile of satisfaction; it was not a very prepossessing place, but they were in no mood to be particular.

'We shall have to report to the Customs Office, shan't we?' inquired Algy.

'Certainly. As a matter of fact we ought to go straight there, but we'll leave it until after we've eaten. I shouldn't be surprised if we are asked some awkward questions. Where's Ginger, by the way?' he added, looking round.

'He stopped at the shop outside to buy a postcard; he said he wanted to send one to his father,' replied Smyth.

'But he hasn't any money, has he?'

'He has a few German marks; he said he thought the people in the shop would change them into Swedish money for him.'

'I see. He's a good kid to think of writing home; it's the last thing a good many would think of at this stage. Well, what are we going to eat? Strewth! Look who's here.'

The glass-topped door of the restaurant had opened, and Blackbeard, with a heavily-built man beside him, entered. Two other men, who may or may not have been with them, followed them in, and seated themselves at a table just inside. Blackbeard, without the slightest hesitation, walked over to the table at which the three Englishmen were sitting, and pulling up a chair from the next table, sat down at Biggles' elbow. The other man did the same.

Biggles did not so much as glance at them. He studied the menu carefully, and then gave an order to the waiter by the simple expedient of pointing on the card to the dishes he chose, although as he confessed to the others, his selection was largely a matter of guess-work.

'There are two things you can always get easily when travelling abroad, whether you speak the language or not,' he said slowly. 'one is food, and the other is the unwelcome attention of strangers.'

'But you wouldn't call me a stranger,' protested Blackbeard evenly.

'I certainly shouldn't include you amongst my friends,' replied Biggles casually. 'My memory is getting bad, I'm afraid, but I cannot recall inviting you to join us at breakfast.'

'No! I thought you might overlook it, so I invited myself,' Blackbeard told him with a curious smile.

'Then I hope you will enjoy watching us eat. We are not really inhospitable, but we are very hungry, so we may be some time. You'll forgive us, I am sure, if we proceed.'

'We are in no hurry. I'll wait for you to finish and then show you what *our* hospitality is like. Make a good meal, we have a long way to go.'

'Really! In that case, why not start?'

'No, we'll wait for you; you're coming with us.'

'Don't you take rather a lot for granted?' observed Biggles, coldly, as he attacked his soup with gusto. Then, with a change of tone, 'Drop the bluff; it won't work here. We're in Sweden now.'

'Bluff?' murmured Blackbeard, raising his eyebrows, and glancing significantly towards the two men just inside the door, and then at several others who could be seen on the pavement outside through the plate-glass windows of the shop front. 'Really, Bigglesworth, you do me less than justice.'

Biggles smiled, but inwardly he knew that the position was more serious than he had at first supposed. It looked as if the crew of the big flying boat had come ashore to support the German, and if that was so, the crew of the Vandal were by no means out of the wood, for Biggles did not need telling that their enemies would stick at nothing to silence them. He saw Ginger walk past the shop front, swing breezily through the door and start towards them, and then hesitate as his eyes fell on Blackbeard. He altered his course abruptly, and without another glance in their direction went straight on through a door at the back of the dining-room that appeared to lead to the rear of the building.

Not by a flicker of an eyelid did Biggles betray that he was one of his party, and Blackbeard, whose back was turned towards the room, did not see him.

Neither Algy nor Smyth had so far taken part in the conversation; they had concentrated their attention on the food that was being set before them with an interest that was by no means feigned. Algy now looked up. 'This is a good pie,' he declared.

'Eat it while you may, my friend,' returned Blackbeard suavely, 'it may be your last.' Then his manner changed. 'I think this has gone on long enough,' he went on coldly. 'In case it is in your minds to do anything foolish, I warn you that it is quite impossible for any of you to leave this room alive except in my company.'

'But you can't—' began Biggles.

Blackbeard waved his hand in a deprecating gesture. 'Can't,' he sneered, 'can't? What word is this? Pish! The issues in which I am interested and in which you have so ill-advisedly meddled, are too big for such words, or to permit a small matter like your removal to stand in the way. Whatever may be demanded as a result of the subsequent investigation, whether it be compensation or merely an apology to the Swedish or even the British Government—these things can be dealt with by those whose work it is. Our object will have been achieved. What has been done cannot be undone. You know too much, Bigglesworth. Incidentally, it may save some unpleasantness if you will return the documents you took from my office.'

For a moment Biggles did not understand, then he remembered the papers that had been in the portfolio which Ginger had taken, and which no doubt still reposed in his pocket. Evidently they were of importance. He looked Blackbeard straight in the face.

'I've no papers of yours,' he said.

Blackbeard shrugged his shoulders. 'Have it that way if you like; it will all be the same in the end,' he said shortly. 'And now, if you have finished your meal, perhaps you are ready to go?'

'Purely as a matter of interest–where?'

'We have a machine waiting,' was the evasive reply.

'In that case I prefer to remain here.'

'As you will. I, however, shall go, so this will be your last opportunity of leaving with safety. Remember that I gave you fair warning. You cannot remain here indefinitely. While you are here you can do no harm; sooner or later you will try to leave, and then–well, my men have their instructions. I might mention that the house is surrounded.'

Biggles lit a cigarette and quietly considered the position, for he knew that Blackbeard was speaking the truth. As the German had said, they knew too much, and they would not be allowed to leave the place alive except to return to Russia. Outrageous though it may seem, murder would be committed. The fact that the murderer, or murderers, might at some future date be apprehended by the police would make no difference as far as they were concerned, or, for that matter, where Russia or Germany were concerned. The governments of those countries would sacrifice the instruments of their nefarious plans without a qualm. The position was desperate, and it was no use blinking at it, he thought. He glanced up at the proprietor of the restaurant who was counting some money on his desk, on which rested a telephone.

'It would be unwise to look for assistance in that direction,' murmured Blackbeard, following his eyes.

'If you attempted to leave this table the move would be your last. My men—'

He was interrupted by a sudden outcry from the door, which was flung open from the outside, and Ginger, followed by half a dozen uniformed policemen, entered.

'There they are!' he cried shrilly, pointing towards the table; 'Those are the fellows who did it.' He indicated Biggles furiously. 'He's the one who's got my purse!'

Before Biggles had time to recover from his astonishment, or Blackbeard to intervene, the policemen had dashed to the table and seized Biggles by the arms.

A man in civilian clothes joined the party, 'I am interpreter,' he said harshly, 'which is Bigglesworth?'

'I am,' replied Biggles quickly, suddenly understanding.

'Yes, that's him—he's the one that's got my money,' joined in Ginger.

'What nonsense is this?' cried Biggles, rising to the occasion. 'I—'

'You better keep explanation for the Chief,' interrupted the interpreter.

The proprietor, the waiters, and even the patrons of the restaurant had by this time all crowded round the scene being enacted at Biggles's table, so it was out of the question for Blackbeard's men to even consider using their weapons. Indeed, in the general scramble it was as much as they could do to see what was going on. Blackbeard himself watched the three prisoners led out through the quickly-growing crowd with impotent rage written on his face.

Through the door and up the street, stared at by

all and sundry, the prisoners were led by their police escort. What happened to Blackbeard they could not see.

'All right, we'll come quietly,' Biggles told the interpreter. 'There is no need for your fellows to wrench my arms off. It's all a mistake; we shan't run away. That's the last thing we should be likely to do,' he added meaningly in an undertone.

The party, still watched by an interested group of spectators, reached an imposing building in the main street and passed through the forbidding portal. There were no formalities; they were hurried along a corridor to the cells, and it was with some satisfaction that they saw they were not to be separated. Biggles laughed as the door clanged behind them—he couldn't help it.

'I've said it before and I'll say it again,' he observed cheerfully, 'that kid's a genius. He's got more "nouse"* than any man I ever met. That idea of his to give us in charge for robbery, and have us led out under police escort, was a brainwave. We were in a nasty jam, and I couldn't see how we were going to get out of it.'

'But this is a bit steep, being clapped into jail,' protested Algy.

'Not so steep as being clapped in a coffin, believe me,' declared Biggles.

* Slang: common sense.

Chapter 15

Biggles Explains

Barely two hours passed before the door was opened by one of the police officers who had arrested them, but he now looked at them with undisguised curiosity as he beckoned them to follow.

They passed up a short flight of stone steps and quickly found themselves in a spacious, well-appointed office. Behind a large mahogany writing-desk near the window sat a broad-shouldered man in uniform, whose natural severity of expression was intensified by piercing blue eyes and close-cropped hair. A little to one side of him sat a man whose black coat and striped trousers were obviously of English cut; a bowler hat rested on the desk in front of him. In an enormous chair at the far side of the room, looking ridiculously out of place, sat Ginger; he grinned sheepishly as they entered.

At a nod from the Chief of Police; for such they rightly judged the uniformed man to be, the policeman who had brought them up departed, leaving the three airmen standing in line in front of the desk. The Commissioner of Police looked at them queerly for a moment, and then said something to the man in the black coat, who cleared his throat and addressed them.

'The Chief does not speak English,' he began, 'so as we assume you do not speak Swedish, I have been asked to talk to you. Which of you is Major Biggles-worth?'

'I am, sir,' replied Biggles.

'And you are the leader of this—er—party?'

Biggles bowed slightly.

'I thought so. My name is Hesterley, and I am personal assistant to Sir Harding Boyce, his Majesty's Consul at Stockholm.'

'Is this Stockholm?' asked Biggles in surprise.

'No, this is Christianbad. I came here as quickly as possible from Stockholm at the request of the Commissioner of Police in response to the pleadings of the junior member of your party, with whom I may say we have already had a conversation. He has explained to me personally his reason for giving you in charge. The Chief'—he glanced at the officer—'has accepted my explanation of the affair, and is satisfied that a mistake has been made. Further, he has been good enough to put a private room at our disposal.The circumstances are extraordinarily difficult, as you will no doubt realize. Whatever the true facts of the case may be, we—that is, my office—can only regard you as ordinary British subjects who have got into trouble, so I must have a full explanation. The police, naturally, will expect a report. You have your passports?'

Biggles took them from his pocket and laid them on the desk. 'My log book is in the machine,' he said,—'you know we came here by air.'

The secretary nodded as he glanced at the passports and handed them on to the Chief. 'We shall have to leave these with the police for the moment,' he said, 'and now, if you don't mind—'

Biggles obediently followed him to a side door into a small waiting-room.

'Now what is all this about?' began the secretary tersely, as the door closed behind them. 'Let me have the facts as quickly and concisely as you can.'

Briefly, sticking only to the main facts, yet omitting nothing of importance, Biggles recounted the events which had resulted in their present predicament.

The secretary watched him closely while he spoke, making a note from time to time in a notebook. 'Perhaps I should not say it, but it seems to me that you have done a good piece of work,' he said softly at the end. 'I have already confirmed your record, and the first part of your story—'

'Confirmed it?'

'Yes. I rang up the Air Ministry. Remember, I have already heard part of the story from that small boy of yours.'

'Of course; I had forgotten.'

'It's deuced awkward, Bigglesworth,' went on the secretary. 'If the Swedish Foreign Office get the hang of this thing, goodness knows where it will end. I have spoken to the Chief, who has already guessed that there is some funny business in the wind and made certain arrangements with him in the interests of all concerned. Nevertheless, he insists—and rightly so—that you must leave the country within twenty-four hours, but it is obviously not safe for you to leave this building at present. The Customs authorities have already gone to fetch your machine from where you left it, and they will take care of it. I will send someone who understands these things to see that the tanks are filled. In the early hours of the morning my car will fetch you, with a diplomatic pass, and take you to

175

your machine. There my responsibility will end, but my advice to you is to get back to England as quickly as possible.'

'I will certainly do that,' declared Biggles.

'You promise?'

'On my word.'

'And you will fly a *direct* course to England–I ask that for special reasons?'

'I will.'

'Good. Head for the Thames and land at Hendon*
–no, don't ask questions–land at Hendon. You will probably receive further instructions when you get there.'

'It shall be as you say.'

'Then that is all, I think; we can't keep the Chief waiting any longer. In your own interests you will have to go back to your–er–room, the four of you, until the time comes for you to leave.'

'Yes, that would be safest. By the way, we have some papers–er–documents—'

'You mean those the boy had?'

'Yes. Did he tell you?'

'I have them.'

'Splendid.. It is a relief to know they are in safe hands.'

'All right, let us go back now. Follow your instructions to the letter and fly direct to England; don't forget that. You will not be really safe until you get there, but if I can do anything else to ensure your safety, you may be sure that I will do it. Please remember that this meeting is unofficial. In my official

---

* R.A.F. Station Hendon, North London. Now the Royal Air Force Museum and open to the public.

capacity I can only wash my hands of the whole thing, but the circumstances are rather unusual. Your German friends will be watched, of course, but no restraint can be placed on their movements. Naturally, the Swedish Government does not want to be involved in trouble with its neighbours.'

'I quite understand that.'

'Well, I'll just have another word with the Chief and then I must leave you. I have made arrangements that you will not want for small luxuries during the rest of the time that you will be here.'

They returned to the larger room where the others were still waiting, and after a short conversation between the secretary and the Chief, which, of course, they did not understand, the Chief pressed a button and their jailer appeared to conduct them back to their cell.

Chapter 16
A One-Sided Fight

It was cold, with a touch of frost in the air, when a knock on the door warned them that the hour for their departure had arrived. They were ready, for they had no luggage to think about, and excitement had prevented them from sleeping except in short, fitful doses.

'Tonight, if all goes well, we shall sleep in our own beds,' said Biggles quietly, 'and I for one shan't be sorry. It seems a long time since I had a full night's rest. Come on, you chaps, here's our escort.'

The door had opened, disclosing the night warden and two men in plain clothes. Not a word passed between any of them as the warden led the way through a long stone corridor, and then up some stairs, stopping at last before what was evidently a side or back door of the police station.

'Der passborts,' was all he said, as he handed Biggles the four slim, blue books, bearing the Royal Arms, in gold, on the front. He opened the door quietly.

'Thank you,' replied Biggles, and followed the two plain-clothes men into a narrow street where a large saloon car was waiting. Without speaking, they took their places, and in a moment were speeding through silent, deserted streets. It was only a short drive to the waterfront, and the car soon pulled up before two massive wooden gates where a policeman stood on duty. He stood aside at a single word from the driver, who indicated to the passengers that the time had come for them to leave the car, and led the way through a small wicket gate into a large, gloomy building, open at the sides, and lighted by a few dingy electric light bulbs. They went straight through it without stopping and emerged on a concrete wharf to which several small motor-boats were moored.

Biggles gave a low exclamation of pleasure as he saw the Vandal, intact and undamaged, amongst them.

'Take a quick look round and see that nothing has been tampered with, and make sure the tanks are full,' he told Smyth in a low voice.

The memory of the gloomy wharf, with its inky water and sombre buildings, was to remain in their memory for a long time. The two plain-clothes men were joined by two night watchmen, and the four of them stood in a little group, silently watching the airmen preparing for their voyage. It was an eerie scene in which every sound was magnified a hundredfold.

The sky was already turning grey by the time they were satisfied with their inspection, and they cast off the mooring rope that held the machine to the wharf. Biggles took his place at the controls.

'We shall kick up a dickens of a din when we start up,' he told Algy quietly. 'If Blackbeard is about he is bound to hear us, but I am afraid that cannot be avoided. The engine will warm up as we taxi out. All right, start up,' he went on more loudly to Smyth, who was standing by the propeller.

The noise, as Biggles had prophesied, was appalling in the restricted area, and the group on the quay put their hands over their ears as they stepped back out

179

of the slipstream as the Vandal swung slowly round to face the wide gates that gave access to the open sea. Biggles waved his hand in silent farewell to the four watchers of their departure, a signal that was acknowledged by a nod from the man who had driven the car; then, giving the engine the throttle in short, sharp bursts, he surged towards the opening.

As they passed the barrier into open water he looked quickly to right and left, and in the dim light saw a small motor-boat shoot out from the shelter of the high sea-wall. It was instinct more than actual thought that made him push the throttle wide open, and it was well that he did so, for even as the Vandal leapt forward under the full power of the propeller, a shot, quickly followed by another, rang out above the noise of the engine. The vicious impact of a bullet somewhere in the tail of the machine reached his ears. He did not pause or even look back, but held the machine, now rapidly gathering flying speed, on its course. At that moment, a weather-stained tramp, with the Russian hammer-and-sickle ensign hanging limply from its peak, churning up a creamy whirlpool of foam under its stern, began to swing round across their path. There was no time to turn. To stop was impossible, for if the pilot throttled back, the impetus of the machine would inevitably carry it nose on into the iron side of the tramp, so he took the only course left open. He jerked the joystick back and literally dragged the Vandal off the water. For one dreadful moment he thought she was going to stall, for she wobbled unsteadily. Had the engine missed at that moment, the end would have been certain, but its rhythmic roar never faltered, and the machine, picking up flying speed, roared over the nose of the steamer, its wing-tips missing the foremast by inches.

Looking down he had a fleeting vision of upturned faces staring at them, and then the danger was passed. He moistened his lips and looked at Algy's white face with a curious smile. 'Closish,' he smiled, as he brought the machine to even keel.

Algy could only nod grimly.

Biggles leaned out of the cockpit and looked behind and below at the fast-receding harbour, still dim in the half light, and saw a motor-boat cutting a white streak of foam across its calm surface. He tried to pick out Blackbeard's machine, but he could not see it, so he turned again and settled down for the long flight that lay before them.

From time to time during the next hour he looked back, but sea and sky were clear and he decided that no pursuit had been attempted. Heading south-west, the Vandal passed over Zeeland and the maze of islands around it. A Heinkel seaplane, bearing the red and white markings of the Royal Danish Air Service, came up and looked at them as they passed over Jutland, but the pilot, after a cheerful wave, which Biggles returned, turned and disappeared into the distance as the cold grey waters of the North Sea loomed up ahead. For a long time they could see the North German and Dutch coastlines in the far distance over their port bow as they struck off on a slightly more southerly course for the mouth of the Thames, but presently they were lost to view as the Vandal stood out over the open sea for England.

The day wore on, and the sun climbed higher and higher into the blue sky, but still the Vandal sped on, the engine purring with the steady beat of a well-oiled sewing machine.

Suddenly Algy, who had been gazing around, touched Biggles lightly on the arm and pointed backward over the tail.

Biggles turned and caught his breath sharply, for dead in line behind them were four aeroplanes. One, which was some distance in front of the other three, was unmistakable; it was Blackbeard's seaplane. It was about three miles away, but after watching it for a few minutes, Biggles knew that it was gaining, as were the other three, which now assumed a military formation.

He looked at Algy with a wry smile, for according to his calculations they were still a good seventy or eighty miles from the English coast. He looked below, but the sea was clear of shipping except for two lonely trawlers which they had already passed, and a smudge of smoke on the far horizon.

Algy raised his eyebrows inquiringly, but Biggles only shrugged his shoulders. There was little he could do except keep straight on, for there was not a cloud in the sky in which they might take cover.

Algy leaned forward until his mouth was near Biggles' ear. 'Where did those other three come from?' he yelled.

'Blackbeard called 'em up by wireless, I expect!' roared Biggles in reply. 'We might have expected it– we had to pass near Germany!'

Algy nodded and turned again to watch the pursuing machines. The formation of three had now caught up with Blackbeard's seaplane and the four of them were not more than a mile behind. 'They'll catch us in about ten minutes,' was his mental note as he sat back in his seat.

The minutes passed slowly. Biggles racked his brain for a solution to the problem, but could find no answer; in the air or on the water, they were completely at the mercy of their opponents. The chatter of a machine-gun made him look round quickly. One of the three machines had outdistanced the others, and, gathering a little altitude, was now coming down on his tail with two long fingers of orange flame spurting from its engine cowling.

Biggles's eyes narrowed. 'You dirty dog,' he thought, 'you'd shoot at an unarmed machine, would you? By James, if I had a gun I'd show you something.' The range was still too long for effective shooting, but there was always a chance of a stray bullet hitting one or the other of them, or disabling the machine. Presently, when the range became shorter, they would certainly be hit if he continued to fly straight, yet his only hope of escape lay in reaching the coast; to land on the open sea would simply provide their enemies with a stationary target at which they could shoot until the machine was sunk or its crew killed. He pushed the joystick forward, determined to hold out as long as possible, and when the worst came to the worst, treat the gunners to a few of the tricks he had learnt in the grim school of war. He took out his revolver and passed it to Algy, not that he expected him to do any serious damage with it, for a revolver against a machine-gun might be compared with a pea-shooter against a rifle. Still, it was better than nothing. He leaned out of the cockpit and saw the leading machine closing in on him. With all his old-time coolness, he watched the gunner's head move forward to peer through the sights, and kicked his rudder bar at the precise moment that the German fired. He smiled

183

grimly as a stream of tracer bullets swept past his wing tip, and the gunner's head jerked up again to discover how his target had vanished so suddenly from his sights.

The distance lessened between them, and the loss of speed occasioned by the manœuvre enabled the other machines to come nearer, one of which went down in a steep dive with the apparent intention of coming up under the Vandal's keel.

Biggles kept them all in view, and as the lower machine came up he flung the Vandal round on its axis and charged straight back through the middle of the formation. The rear machine got in a fleeting shot at him as he passed, and a bullet whanged against the Vandal's engine cowling, but it did no damage. Algy had fired, too, but without visible result. Again Biggles turned, and, thrusting the stick hard forward, snatched a lead of nearly a quarter of a mile before the other pilots had grasped his intention. He knew it was only postponing the end, for such manœuvres could not go on indefinitely, and he could not hope to be successful every time, yet it was better than doing nothing.

The gunners, with their greatly superior speed, were on him again almost at once, like a pack of wolves on the trail of a wounded doe, and again he had to swerve wildly to dodge the leaden hail. It cost him a certain amount of valuable height, but it was unavoidable. His lips became a straight line as the gunners, gaining experience by their previous failures, opened out and prepared to come in from each side and below at the same time, and he held the stick tightly, determined that if the Vandal was hit in a vital place, he would at least take one of them crashing down to oblivion with him.

Something—it may have been a flash of his old war-time intuition—made him look up, and he stiffened, staring unbelievingly. He jabbed Algy in the ribs with his elbow and pointed. Six all-metal Nimrods*, bearing the red, white and blue insignia of the Royal Air Force, their gleaming cowlings half hidden behind the whirling discs of their propellers, were screaming down in a wing-tip to wing-tip dive. As they neared the Vandal the formation broke like a bursting rocket and the separate machines took up positions around the travel-stained amphibian. Biggles looked at them wonderingly, marvelling at their sudden appearance. Then he saw and understood. Far away, almost on the horizon, was the squat, ugly outline of an aircraft-carrier heading towards them at full speed, two great feathers of spray leaping from her knife-like bows. Something told him that its appearance had not been simply a lucky fluke. What was it Hesterley had said? 'If I can do anything more to ensure your safety, I will.' He must have rung up the Air Ministry on the telephone, or got in touch with them by wireless, and the carrier was the answer.

He looked behind, but Blackbeard and his three companions were already mere specks in the distance, racing nose down for home. The Nimrods had made no attempt to pursue them; the safety of the British machine was their only consideration. He caught Algy's eye and grinned, and then waved to the pilot of the nearest machine, who had pushed up his goggles,

---

* Hawker Nimrod, a single seat biplane fighter, armed with 2 machine guns, used by the Royal Navy in the early 1930s.

disclosing the smiling face of a lad of about eighteen. 'Good old England,' he thought soberly, 'you certainly turned up trumps at the crucial moment that time.'

A dark, low-lying shadow appeared on the skyline, and he knew that it was the English coast.

The Nimrods stayed with them until the estuary of the Thames opened out below, and then, reverting to their flight formation, dived a parting salute and disappeared in the direction of their parent ship which had been left far behind. Half an hour later the Vandal's wheels rumbled over the famous Royal Air Force aerodrome at Hendon and rolled to a standstill in front of the hangars. An N.C.O.* in slate-blue uniform detached himself from a little group of mechanics and hurried towards it.

'Major Bigglesworth, sir?' he asked Biggles, who was stiffly removing his flying cap.

'Yes?'

'Would you be good enough to come with me, sir—to the Air Ministry? I have a car waiting.'

'Do you want us all to come?'

'Nothing was said about anyone else, sir. There's a party here to take charge of the machine,' he added, glancing critically at the dirtiest aeroplane he had ever seen in his life.

'She looks as if a wash and brush up wouldn't do her any harm,' smiled Biggles as he jumped down from the cockpit.

'That's what I was thinking, sir,' laughed the N.C.O.

'Just give me a minute and I'll be with you,' Biggles told him, and then to Algy, 'I suppose the Air Ministry

---

* Non-commissioned Officer i.e. a Sergeant or a Corporal.

wants a full report of the whole thing, and one of us will be sufficient. You'd better take Smyth and Ginger along to your rooms, and I'll join you as soon as I can get away. We'll leave the machine here for the present.'

Algy nodded. 'Good enough,' he agreed, 'we'll go home and wait for you.'

Chapter 17

The Raiders' Fate

It was nearly nine o'clock that night, however, before Biggles joined the others at Algy's flat in a side turning off Baker Street. He found them yawning in their chairs with the debris of a meal on the table in front of them.

'Anything left?' he asked, glancing at the remnants.

'We've had bacon and eggs. How will that suit you?' replied Algy.

'Fine. Pour me out a cup of that coffee and I'll tell you the rest of the story; it won't take long.'

'Go ahead,' answered Algy, passing the coffee.

Biggles lit a cigarette and threw the dead match into the fireplace. 'Have you seen an evening paper by any chance?' he inquired.

Algy shook his head.

'I thought not or you'd have had more to say when I came in. Well, it's all over.'

'What's all over?'

'The Russian Air Fleet. It isn't any more–or not much of it. It's busted wide open.'

'Come on, out with it!' cried Algy impatiently. 'What's happened?'

'Well, this is the story as far as I can make it out,' went on Biggles, 'although you must understand that the Air Ministry are not saying much about it; I've had to guess part of it, although they helped me with a few broad hints. This was the order of it, and it all hung on those papers Ginger snaffled in Russia. As far as I remember, not one of us looked at them, although it wouldn't have mattered very much if we had, as they were in Russian, but they meant a dickens of a lot to that fellow we met in Christianbad—what was his name—Hesterley. He sent the whole story to England in code while we were kicking our heels in that cell. No wonder Blackbeard was upset.' Biggles dropped his voice to a dramatic whisper.

'Last night was the night decided for a full dress rehearsal of the Russian Air Fleet's raid on Great Britain; thirty flying boats were to take part, landing at nine different bases on the English coast. The numbers of the machines and the exact positions of the objectives, were all set out in those papers, together with the names of the people taking part, and all the rest of it. Each pilot was issued with a copy, and I can only suppose that Blackbeard was so scared when he found his was missing that he did not dare to report their loss, but tried to get them back in his own way, or at least prevent us from getting back. He is certainly going to be out of luck if he ever returns to Russia. Well, there was the story, and the Air Ministry wasted no time. As far as can be at present ascertained, only two of those machines succeeded in getting back to the base in Russia. Some were damaged, and must have gone down in the North Sea trying to get back; one, they say, is down on the Dutch coast. The evening papers have got hold of a story about a lot of mysterious aircraft wreckage being washed up here and there on the East Coast. The Ministry have denied any knowledge of the matter to the press, as they were bound to without running the risk of starting a war, and; as a matter of fact, they've succeeded in hushing the thing up pretty well. The newspapers have guessed that there is a lot more behind it, of course, but in the national interest they are allowing the thing to drop.'

'But what happened?' cried Algy.

Biggles shook his head. 'I doubt if we shall ever know for certain, but a wink is as good as a nod to a blind horse, and I have my own opinion.'

'You think—'

'I believe that as soon as our people got the word, they made a lightning raid on every base that had been laid down in this country. Not only were the bases named in the papers, but there was a map marking their exact positions. Well, they collared the whole works, and quite a number of the personnel, I believe; they will probably be deported in due course. Every one of the black flying boats–or, I should say, nearly every one–crashed on landing, and that to my mind can only have been brought about by one thing. The submerged lights must have functioned, or the pilots would not have attempted to land; but I should say they functioned in the wrong places.'

'You mean–our people shifted them?'

'Exactly. The lights were switched on, but instead of the illuminated positions being nice sheltered coves, they were amongst shoal, sand and rocks. You can imagine what happened. The machines would either buckle up or tear their keels out when they bumped into *terra firma*. They would certainly stick if they did not actually crash, and I expect our people were watching to pick up the survivors. Mind you, this is only assumption on my part, but I know for a fact that the machines all piled up where they came down, and that is the only way I can account for it. It seems a bit drastic, I must admit, but when all is said and done, the treatment handed out to these fellows was nothing like as drastic as that which they would have handed out to us when the time was ripe. There is not the slightest doubt that at some date in the near future it was intended to blow England out of the water by wholesale bombing.'

'I always realized that that was the ultimate idea,' agreed Algy. 'They've got what they asked for, and they'll think twice before they try anything like that again. Was that all they said at the Air Ministry?'

'Pretty well. I made a full and complete report which was taken down in writing by a shorthand typist. At the finish I was thanked by the Chief of the Air Staff on behalf of the Secretary of State for Air–which, of course, means the Government–and asked to extend their thanks to my "gallant and duty-devoted comrades." '

'Was that all?' asked Algy bluntly. 'Didn't they even offer to pay our expenses? This trip has cost a bit of money one way and another.'

A slow smile spread over Biggles's face as he slowly took an envelope from his pocket. 'You do me less than justice, as our friend Blackbeard would say,' he said reprovingly. 'I have a cheque which makes rather good reading, to be divided between you and I in such proportions as we may decide, being the chief partners in the affair so to speak. There is a further cheque for £500 for Smyth, to do what he likes with, and another for the same amount for this ginger-headed young rascal–wait a minute, my lad, I haven't finished yet–in *my* name, to be devoted to his education in any way that I may think fit. As an alternative, if he prefers it, the Service will take charge of him, in which case he will proceed to Cranwell* as an aircraft apprentice. Which is it to be, Ginger?'

'Do I have any say in my education?' asked Ginger shrewdly.

'Within reason. What's your idea of it?'

'To go to a civil flying school and get my tickets– flying and ground engineer's licences.'

'That's all right with me. You can go down to Brooklands and start in as soon as you like. You may learn to fly, but you won't be able to take your tickets just yet because you're still under age.'

'Never mind that; as long as I can fly, that's all I care. When I get my hands on a joystick I shall be able to hold my own with you guys on the next show we do.'

'Well, I'm taking the Vandal down to Brooklands tomorrow for a complete overhaul; I'll take you down with me if you like,' concluded Biggles.

'OK big boy!' cried Ginger enthusiastically.

* An R.A.F. station used for training.